THE
INTERNATIONAL
YETI
COLLECTIVE
SHADOWSPRING

For David Mason
1938–2019
Grandfather, potter, tiddlywinker
– PM

To Harry
– KR

STRIPES PUBLISHING LIMITED
An imprint of the Little Tiger Group
1 Coda Studios, 189 Munster Road,
London SW6 6AW

www.littletiger.co.uk

First published in Great Britain by Stripes Publishing Limited in 2020
Text copyright © Paul Mason, 2020
Illustrations copyright © Katy Riddell, 2020

ISBN: 978-1-78895-181-4

A CIP catalogue record for this book is available from the British Library.

Printed and bound in the UK.

2 4 6 8 10 9 7 5 3 1

PAUL MASON

KATY RIDDELL

THE
INTERNATIONAL
YETI
COLLECTIVE

SHADOWSPRING

LITTLE TIGER
LONDON

Tadpole *(she of unripe character)* gripped a hollowed-out reed between her teeth and eyed the long trench of muddy slop in front of her. She darted forwards and launched herself into the air, arms outstretched. As she hit the sludge with a splat, Tadpole heard the Greybeards on the banks break into a cheer, then she plunged under the blanket of mud. Tadpole blew out a blast of air to clear her snorkel and began to move – wiggling her body from side to side, arms pinned and legs flailing. It had been a while since she last slop-snorkelled and she was a little out of practice.

As Tadpole took deep breaths through the reed, she hoped she was near the finish line. But, with eyes clamped shut, it was impossible to tell. She carried on, her back aching, until at last she felt her head bump against the end of the channel.

Tadpole pushed herself up and raised a fist, expecting

cheers and happy yodelling from the spectators, but there was silence. She tilted her head to both sides to clear her ears, then wiped the mud from her eyes.

Shipshape *(she in perfect order)* stood on the bank, the Stinking Sash of the silverback across her chest, her face lined with exasperation. Beside her stood Rainstorm the Guardian *(he of damp humour)*, shaking his head – his thin, sinewy arms folded over the beard that hung down his chest. The other yeti in the slop room shuffled uneasily and stared at their toes.

The silverback squinted at the pool. "Is that you, Tadpole?"

Tadpole heaved one leg over, then the other. She struggled to her feet, mud oozing from her fur into a giant puddle on the ground, and took the breathing tube out of her mouth. "Mum! We were just making sure the slopping trench was all good to go … for when the visitors arrive."

"Really?" said Shipshape. "I asked you younglings to fill the trench with fresh mud, smooth it over, and then make the seats comfortable with new moss." Shipshape pointed to the rows of wooden viewing benches that rose up on one side of the room. "You were supposed to get a Greybeard game ready for our guests from the Collective."

"Not dive into the mud like piglets." Rainstorm glared round the room. "We could hear you in the Council chambers!"

"We were just testing it out," Tadpole ventured.

"You were just *mucking* about," said Shipshape. "You've made a terrible mess."

Tadpole glanced at the room, now covered in mud splats. Perhaps she should have thought twice about the dive and started from inside the trench the way you were supposed to.

"We'll clean it up right away, and get that moss spread in a jiffy," said Slapstick *(he who trips over his own feet)*. The other younglings nodded hurriedly.

"Please see that you do," said Shipshape.

"And their punishment, O Shipshape?" asked Rainstorm, gesturing at the younglings with his staff.

"That's enough, I think."

Rainstorm gave an exasperated snort. "Might I suggest—"

"Thank you, Guardian, that is all."

"As you wish." Rainstorm glowered at the young Greybeards. "Just make sure you're done before last horn, or I will come looking for you."

"Why not return to the Council chambers, Rainstorm? I'll meet you there," said Shipshape.

The Guardian gave a bow and swept out into the corridor.

"A quiet word, please." Shipshape beckoned Tadpole over. Tadpole sighed and followed her mother out of the slop room.

Shipshape stroked the long hairs on her chin, silky and grey. She looked weary, thought Tadpole, there was a melancholy to her eyes. "You know how busy I am now, don't you? With the Gathering upon us? The ambassadors are due to set off soon – any moon!"

"Sorry, Mum." Tadpole could guess what was coming next.

"Look, I know it's not easy being the daughter of the silverback, but you've got to start acting your age," said Shipshape. "You're not a fledgling any more."

"I know." Tadpole recited the next words in her head – she knew exactly what her mother would say. *Believe it or not, one day this sett will look to you for answers…*

"Believe it or not, one day this sett will look to you for answers, my love," said Shipshape. "And you'll need to be ready."

Tadpole's voice dropped to a whisper. "I get it."

Shipshape brushed away a glob of mud from the fur on Tadpole's face. "Do you?"

"I get it," said Tadpole, this time with a faint smile.

Shipshape leaned in and fluttered her eyelashes against Tadpole's cheek. "Now go and wash yourself off, then come back to help the others. I'll see you at rehearsal later." She closed her eyes and pinched the bridge of her nose.

"You OK, Mum?"

5

"Fine," said Shipshape, turning to leave.

Tadpole went to the waterfall room and stood under the trickle of water falling through the rock, hoping some of the embarrassment would wash off too. She thought about the pressure that her mother was under – now more than ever. The canoes of the International Yeti Collective would arrive before long. It was the first Gathering of the nineteen yeti setts for as long as anyone could remember. The Almas, the Mande Barung, the Sasquatch, the Makimaki and more were all sending their ambassadors.

Tadpole didn't know much about the other yeti – they all lived so far away. But *everyone* knew about the Mountain Yeti and their brave expedition – the story carried across the world by bat messengers. It had been all anyone talked about for moons! How a gang of humans stole the Mountain Yeti slabs – the ancient carvings that recorded the history of the yeti, every yeti law and, more worryingly, the whereabouts of every yeti sett. (Tadpole knew the Greybeards had their own copy, carved in oak, resting on a bed of heather in the Council chambers.)

With the ancient slabs in the hands of the humans, every sett across the globe had been in danger. It could have spelled the end of the yeti way of life. But the Mountain Yeti didn't hide. Instead, they crossed the Earth, paddling along underground waterways, tracked down the thieves and then took the slabs away before the humans had a chance to work out what they said. Barrelling down rivers, having adventures, embracing new things. *Now that's how to live*, thought Tadpole.

The daring exploits of the Mountain Yeti had also brought the Collective back to life.

In Greybeard school, you learned about the time when the setts of the Collective had worked together like the threads of a spider's web: all joined in one purpose – to care for the Earth. But, over time, the web started to fall apart. Although each sett still carried out their chosen role, without links between them, the net had grown weak.

At the same time, the humans grew stronger and the world began to tremble under their feet. People filled the sky with smoke from their contraptions, turned rivers and oceans foul with their filth, chopped down trees and drove animals from their homes. Worst of all, under their watch, the world became warmer and warmer still. No one knew how it would end.

"So much is at stake," Shipshape had said in her speech to the sett just the other moon. "We need a strong Collective now more than ever. How do we fix things? Do we work with humans or against them?"

It was a question the Gathering would try to answer. Tadpole knew it was a real honour for their little sett, the Greybeards, to be hosting ambassadors from the entire

Collective. As leader of the sett, Shipshape was desperate to make sure everything ran as smoothly as possible. With a pang, Tadpole realized that she hadn't exactly helped. She shook the water from her fur and padded back into the slop room.

"Another one of your brilliant ideas, Tadpole." Tagalong *(she who always follows)* scrubbed the walls with a cloth. "Last time I listen to you."

"Rainstorm was super cross," said Slapstick.

"He's always cross," said Tagalong.

"I probably should have thought that dive through a little more," Tadpole admitted. "Sorry."

"Come on then, give us a hand … Piglet," said Tagalong with a grin.

"Don't you start." Tadpole grabbed a mop and got to work on the floor.

At the sound of last horn, Tadpole helped Tagalong
and Slapstick pack everything up, and padded along the
tunnel in a hurry. She passed by the firefly nursery, lit
up like sunlight, the keepers coaxing the little flies into
their lanterns, then the apothecary's chamber, with its
strange jars of roots, herbs and wriggling bugs. At last, she
stopped on Potters' Path, the potters still at work, wheels
turning, the shelves lining the walls full of fresh plates,
cups and jugs drying.

Tadpole gazed at the potters, watching in quiet wonder
as bowls rose out of the spinning mud, edges climbing
from under their gentle fingers. It wasn't that long ago
that Snowdrift *(he with white fur)* would have been at his
wheel, hands cupping a lump of pale clay. Tadpole had
always been in awe of Grandfather's touch – so soft, so
watchful, bringing the wet mud into being as if by magic.

And now he had passed on. Tadpole felt for the clay pendant that hung around her neck as she so often did. Touching it made him feel close – as if he was still there with her – and Tadpole liked to hear his voice.

"*Ah, my favourite grandfluff.*" Snowdrift appeared at the wheel, his eye on a spinning pot.

"I'm your only grandfluff."

Grandfather grinned from beneath his snowy beard. "*That must be why you're my favourite. Any particular reason you have mud behind your ears?*" he asked, lifting his hands away, and letting the wheel slow down. Satisfied, he glanced up.

Tadpole scratched the back of her head, looking sheepish.

"*Don't tell me, I can guess.*" Snowdrift chuckled. "*Another fine mess, eh?*"

"Something like that. Mum told me off."

"*Then perhaps you should stop doing things to upset her.*"

"Are you all right, Tadpole?" Tadpole turned to see her dad, Waterworks *(he who often sheds tears)*, standing there with a puzzled look on his face.

Tadpole realized she was staring at an empty potter's wheel. "Fine, Dad."

Waterworks followed her gaze. "You miss Grandfather. It still hurts, I know. But I believe he's very much here." He placed a warm palm against Tadpole's cheek. Tadpole could see his eyes glistening.

"Thanks, Dad." Tadpole wiped away a tear as it crept down her father's fur.

"*My son's right, you know*," Snowdrift chortled.

Waterworks cleared his throat. "Now we'd better get a move on – it's almost time for rehearsal."

★

Tadpole and Waterworks arrived at the giant meeting hall to find it filled with happy yodelling and chitchat. As they nattered, the Greybeards stroked their extravagant whiskers – some reaching almost to their knees, mustachios spreading from their mouths like overhanging vines. Tadpole felt her own face, still a little embarrassed that she was yet to have anything more than the most modest beard. From the open kitchen door across the hall wafted the wonderful smell of sizzling pine weevils. Tadpole caught sight of a giant pot overflowing with sauce, and frying pans sitting on top of bubbling thermal mud, as cooks bustled about in their aprons.

Even with all the commotion, Tadpole heard her dad's stomach let out a large gurgle. "Hope it doesn't go on for ages – I'm starving!" said Waterworks.

"You're always starving."

Waterworks shrugged. "That is true."

At the front of the cave, Shipshape stood with the choir leader, Upstage *(she who demands attention)*, trying to cajole the rowdy horde into rows with a loudhailer fashioned out of rolled-up tree bark. "Come on, you scallywags, get to your places!" she called. "No, not just you, Scallywag. I mean everyone in general." Scallywag *(he who is naughty)* grinned from behind his enormous beard and gave her a wave.

"We'll never get anywhere at this rate," said Upstage.

Rainstorm thumped his staff on the floor once, twice, three times, and the Greybeards fell silent under his glare. The gathering quickly assembled into their lines.

Shipshape straightened the sash across her chest. "Thank you, Greybeards. Let's not waste any more time. Before we can have dinner, we need to get this welcome performance right for when the Collective begin to gather. Really put your hearts into it, yes? Remember: *great oaks from little acorns grow.*"

"From the top, if you please. The greeting song: 'You Know What They Say'."

Upstage waved her arms and counted them in…

You know what they say…

Hold the stone as one and it won't feel heavy,
A good buttock deserves a comfortable seat,
With patience the ant can eat an elephant.
Oh, listen to this wise drumbeat.

12

The dropping never falls far from the pigeon,
The first pancake is always a mess,
No toad comes to light without reason,
To all this and more I profess.

When warthogs fight, it is the grass that suffers,
A shrimp that sleeps gets carried by the tide,
Every vegetable has its season, its season.
Let these words be your faithful guide.

A big chair does not make a leader,
The sun which melts wax hardens clay,
Even a tiny star shines in the darkness,
You know, that's just what they say,

You know, that's just what they say…

Upstage gave a warm round of yodelling. "Lovely, lovely," she crowed. The Greybeards looked at each other, beaming, and the choir leader took them through the song twice more.

"All good things come to those who wait – now let's eat!" said Shipshape to a happy roar.

The kitchen crew wasted no time, and quickly filed in with plates of pine-weevil flan and jugs of worm sauce.

Shipshape came over to join her family.

13

"Hey, Mum." Tadpole leaned over and gave her a nuzzle.

"You look exhausted," said Waterworks.

"I could really use some food," agreed Shipshape. She dug her fingers into her flan and lifted some to her mouth. "Mmm. So how was everyone's moon?"

"All hands to the pump." Waterworks poured out a large helping of worm sauce.

"Then perhaps you could go down to Shadowspring next moon and help out, Tadpole," said Shipshape.

"But it's my shadow-puppet play for the fledglings in the morning. The one I've been rehearsing for ages." Tadpole put down her weevil pastry.

Shipshape flinched. "Oh yes, of course."

"You said you'd try to come this time, Mum. Remember?"

"I remember."

"*Mum!*" Tadpole groaned.

"I'll be there." Shipshape held up her hands.

"We'll both find a way to be there," agreed Dad, wiping drops of gravy from his chin.

Over Dad's shoulder Tadpole spied Rainstorm and his son Butterfingers *(he lumbering and clumsy)* squeezing their way through the crowded hall.

Rainstorm bowed to them. "Just wanted to wish you a good evening on our way out and remind you that we're meeting all the farmers and growers first thing."

"Ah yes, about that." Shipshape glanced over at Tadpole. "As it happens, I need to be at Tadpole's shadow play in the morning."

"Play?" asked Butterfingers.

"I put on shadow-puppet shows for the fledglings at school," Tadpole explained. "You can come, if you like."

Butterfingers shook his huge head. "Sorry, Tadpole. I'm helping in the quarry. Dad says."

"Doing his bit." Rainstorm patted him on the shoulder fondly. "They grow up so fast. His beard will be full before we know it."

"Isn't that the truth!" said Shipshape.

Rainstorm turned to Tadpole. "And what about you? Did you clean up that terrible mess of your own making?"

"All gone," said Tadpole.

Shipshape gave an embarrassed smile. "Now about the meeting…"

"Not to worry, Shipshape. I'll take care of it. Happy to run things in your absence," said Rainstorm.

Shipshape let out a relieved sigh. "I don't know what I'd do without you by my side, Rainstorm. I'll be there as soon as I can."

"Good luck with your play, Tadpole," said Butterfingers as they left.

"That Butterfingers is a nice youngling, isn't he?"

Shipshape dropped the last bit of flan into her mouth and pushed her plate away. She let out a long sigh and rubbed her temples.

"You OK?" asked Waterworks.

"I think I might turn in early."

Waterworks got to his feet. "I'll come with you. Tadpole, be a good Greybeard and clear for us?"

"Yes, Dad."

Tadpole waited for them to go. "I can't believe Mum totally forgot about my play," she muttered as she stacked the plates.

Snowdrift emerged at her side. "*She is extremely busy at the moment.*"

"It's not just that. Mum doesn't think the future silverback should waste time on shadows," said Tadpole. "But I'm not like her. I'm no leader."

"*You just might surprise yourself one moon, Tadpole,*" said Snowdrift.

"Do you think Mum is still cross with me about the peak-running thing?"

"*You mean when you disappeared for a full moon to explore the valley of the humans without telling anyone, and the whole sett panicked?*"

"Hey, it's hardly my fault this place is so boring."

Snowdrift chortled. "*You don't need to explain yourself to me – follow your bliss, I always say.*"

"But you're coming to my performance, right?"

"*As long as you want me there,*" said Snowdrift. "*Now how about a game of yettiwinks before nesting? Got to keep my eye in — I'm still the best in the sett.*"

"You've passed on, remember," Tadpole chuckled.

"*That's no excuse.*"

★

Back in the family den, Tadpole brought out the lichen mat, a clay pot, her squidger piece and a handful of little coloured discs, setting them up on the slab. She got herself a cup of gorse juice, and soon she and Snowdrift were pressing down with their squidgers, making the little winks click and jump in the air, trying to get them to land in the empty pot. It was Grandfather and Grandfluff playing together again, thought Tadpole, the way it had so often been during her fledgling years.

"*Blast!*" hissed Snowdrift as one of his winks flew off the bench and disappeared into thin air. He covered his mouth.

Tadpole was puzzled. "Blast?"

"*It's what you say if you're cross about something.*" Snowdrift dropped his voice to a whisper. "*It's a Hazel word.*"

"A Hazel word."

Hazel. Human Hazel. Grandfather's dear friend. That

was how he put it. *Dear friend.* For a Greybeard to even think of a human in that way was unheard of.

Though humans had once been their cousins, now yeti avoided them at all costs. So much so that the Greybeards even had a way to scare them off the ranges: Murmuring.

Tadpole knew how to Murmur – every Greybeard did. It was just part of who you were, like a cat purring or the bellow of a reindeer. A Murmur began with a vibration, deep in your chest, which started low, rising higher and higher, up through your jaw, making your teeth hum, and then out through your nostrils as a buzz. Not a loud, cheerful buzz like that of a bee, but a soft, almost imperceptible drone, mournful and troubling. Humans couldn't even hear it – but they could certainly feel it. And, when humans felt a Murmur, they ran, as if their very lives were at stake, often with a strangled cry caught in their throats – or so Tadpole had heard. She'd never Murmured (properly, that is, at humans). It was only ever meant to be used when all else failed and your back was against the rock.

Yes, humans and Greybeards did not mix. And to go anywhere near a human dwelling and meet one the way Snowdrift had done? You'd be banished from the sett before your hairy feet had a chance to touch the ground – your name wiped from memory.

But that didn't stop a Greybeard like Snowdrift.

Tadpole knew the story well. How Grandfather had tripped and tumbled down the hill and into Hazel's life all those cycles ago. How their paths had literally collided. It was the start of an unusual bond that lasted a lifetime. Yetisitting Tadpole in the family den, Snowdrift had often spoken of the times he visited Hazel's dwelling in secret – of their companionship. How he made a grave for her when she passed away and laid her to rest. From time to time, Grandfather even taught Tadpole the little human tongue he knew.

Hazel had been Grandfather's secret. But Snowdrift shared it with her so that Tadpole would understand that humans could be decent folk too. Tadpole sometimes wished he'd never told her at all. It would have been easier to grow up suspicious of people, like every other Greybeard. But instead she had to keep it hidden inside. And now, with Grandfather gone, she was on her own.

Tadpole pushed down on one of her winks and watched it miss the pot completely.

"Blast," she said under her breath.

"That can't be much fun by yourself." Dad came from the bedroom and nodded at the empty seat opposite her. "I could give you a round or two?"

Tadpole pressed down and shot a second wink straight into the pot. "You're going down, Dad."

Henry Wetwood stared through his dorm-room window
at the dark mountains looming over Halbrook Hall.
Strands of cloud stole down from the ranges and drifted
through the forest. In the fading light, the walls of his
new boarding school looked stained and grim, dotted with
weathered crests, and rising to battlements like a castle.
In the grounds was an equally gloomy cottage, with a sign
that read **HEAD   STER'S   ESID NCE**. Halbrook
Hall looked nothing like the sunny pictures on the
website. Just where had he come to?

   It had only been a couple of hours since Mum and Dad
dropped him off, but already it seemed like a lifetime, and
the gnawing ache in Henry's chest threatened to grow
into full-blown misery. Apart from a two-day school camp
last year, he'd hardly ever been away from home on his
own before.

Henry busied himself making his bed, hastily covering the threadbare mattress that was slumped across the wooden frame. He unpacked the last of the books he'd managed to squeeze into his suitcase, and arranged his boxes of Vault and Serpent cards on the shelf by his bed.

Seeing the cards made him think of sitting round a table with David and Li, his best mates from his old school, deep in a game. They hadn't taken it very well when he'd told them that he was going.

"Mountains? Boarding school? Boys only … no girls? You're kidding!" Li said. "What about Wi-Fi? Do they even have that?"

"Of course they have Wi-Fi," Henry snorted, although he didn't know for certain.

"Why are you even going?" asked David.

"I told you, Mum and Dad will be in Hungary."

"Then they should just eat," David chuckled. His smile faded when he saw the pained look on Li and Henry's faces.

"Never tell that joke again," said Li.

"Fair enough," said David.

Henry told them all about Béla Karman, a famous Hungarian author, and his first new book in thirty years – and how he'd chosen the Wetwoods to publish it. "Dad says it's a masterpiece, a bestseller. It's going to save our publishing business."

"I still don't understand where boarding school comes in," said David.

"Well, this Karman guy's a genius, but a bit eccentric – he wants Mum and Dad to stay out there with him in his farmhouse in the middle of nowhere in Hungary – but just Mum and Dad. He won't have it any other way," explained Henry. "They have to go there for six months."

"And so you're off to boarding school," said Li.

Henry sighed. "Dad reckons it'll be good for me – he went to boarding school at my age."

"Maybe you could come and stay with me instead," said David.

Henry pictured David's small room, crammed with untidy bunks, three brothers sharing. "They already enrolled me – thanks anyway."

"But you're our Vault Master," Li complained. She gestured at the neat rows of cards spread out on the table.

"It won't be forever. We'll just have to put the campaign on hold. Maybe we can play online?" Henry laid down a card. "Tollbridge Ogre ready to attack! How do you answer, Warlock Jones?"

"Interesting." David examined the cards in his hand and chose one with a wand on it. "I cast a vanishing spell." He picked up the dice and rolled.

"Twenty!" Henry turned his ogre face down. "Ogre defeated."

"Nice try," said David.

"And what about our eco club at school?" asked Li. "Elf Queen Li observes the battlefield." She rolled a six.

"I'll be back to help soon, I promise." Henry looked at the campaign table and thought for a moment. "Queen Li, you see a path into the woods, but you are not sure where it leads."

"But Queen Li uses her map," Li declared, playing a card with a picture of a map on it. "She advances into the woods."

"Nice," said David.

Li shook her head. "Boarding school, really? It sounds so Harry Potter."

"Let's hope so," said Henry.

★

With the clanging of an old hand bell, Henry's roommate, Murray, came back to their room to get him for dinner. Swamped by a blazer many sizes too big, his shirt collar dwarfing a thin neck, Murray seemed just as nervous as Henry for someone who wasn't even a new boy.

"What are all those?" asked Murray, pointing at the boxes.

"Vault and Serpent." Henry showed his best wizard card.

Murray shrugged. "Never played it. What do you have to do?"

23

Henry shuffled through his pack, telling Murray about adventurers and friendship and noble quests. Of crossing paths with wonderful beasts and thwarting villains. He showed Murray the game board and notebooks. "I can teach you how to play later, if you like?"

"Great. It's been ages since I played a board game. Got a few at home, but Dad can't be bothered with games."

"My dad tried to join a campaign with me and my mates once. But he was hopeless," said Henry.

"At least he tried, right?" said Murray. "Come on or we'll be late."

★

The dining hall was a huge old room filled with shadows. Lights hung from the lofty ceiling, but half of them didn't seem to be working. The room was full of loud talk and the clank and scrape of cutlery on metal dinner trays, but at least the food looked edible – some sort of stew with potatoes, and sponge cake swimming in custard.

Once they'd jostled their way to the front of the queue and thanked the cooks as they slopped out the food, Henry trailed behind Murray to the end of a long table. From there, they could see out over the sports fields to the woods beyond.

Henry was relieved that his arrival barely attracted any attention at all. He was quite happy to be invisible – he didn't feel much like talking. Mrs Nettles, the house parent – a broad-shouldered woman in a tweed jacket – sat at her own small table. She gave him a quick smile and that was that.

Henry realized that he was starving and started hastily tucking in. As he was finishing, most of the boys were already back in the queue for more.

"You need to be quick around here if you want seconds," said the boy sitting opposite. "I'm Stuart, but everyone calls me Bony."

"Henry." He offered his hand. Bony reached over and shook it.

"New, eh?"

Henry wiped Bony's gravy off his fingers and nodded.

"I was new once." Bony scraped the last of the custard from his tray and eyed the servery, but the cooks were already packing the pots away.

Henry glanced round the dining hall. At the far end of the room sat a group of older boys, leaning back in their chairs.

"Senior prefects," said Murray, following his gaze.

Henry watched as one of the boys in the middle of the group, his hair towering in an oily quiff, beckoned towards the neighbouring table and pointed at his tray. Moments later, a team of younger boys started to clear the prefects' table, taking the trays, scraping the leftover food into the bin, and stacking them by the kitchen door.

Henry pushed his tray away and pulled out his phone, resting it on his lap, hoping to see a message from Mum and Dad, but he couldn't get a signal.

"Put that away," hissed Murray. "I can give you the Wi-Fi password back in our room."

Henry shoved the phone back in his pocket, but at the same time felt a tap on his shoulder. He looked up to see the prefect with the quiff standing over him. "No mobiles in the dining hall."

"He didn't know," said Murray. "He's new."

"I can see that." The boy pinched the fabric of Henry's blazer. "What's your name?"

"Henry Wetwood." Henry tried to keep the warble out of his voice.

"In with you, is he, Murray Mint?" The boy turned to Murray. "Didn't you tell him that a phone in the dining hall is instant confiscation and detention?"

Henry gulped. "It won't happen again."

The boy paused, running a hand through his hair. "Well, seeing as it's your first day…" he said at last.

"Thanks," said Henry.

"But you owe me," said the boy.

"That's Fraser Ragbone, the head boy," Murray said, as soon as the prefect had left.

"I'm glad I don't owe him a favour," said Bony.

"Shush, Bony," said Murray.

★

Back in his room after evening prep Murray rummaged around in his desk drawer and gave a piece of printed paper to Henry. "Here's that Wi-Fi password."

"Thanks." Henry pulled out his phone and tapped in the code. His heart lifted to see a notification.

Writing this on the train back to London. Hope you're settling in all right and your room-mate is nice. (Dad says he had three room-mates squeezed into one room his first year!) I wish we could have stayed a bit longer to see you settled – it all felt so rushed. But you'll like boarding school, Dad and I are sure of it. The months will fly by, you'll see.

Anyway, our flight is tomorrow – excited about meeting Karman and working on the book. Chat when we can. Miss you.

Love Mum and Dad xxx

Henry started writing back. At first, he tapped out everything that was going on in his head – how lonely he felt, how awful Halbrook was, his smelly mattress, the prefects. Couldn't they turn round and come and get him? But then he imagined their faces when they read all that and deleted the message. He started again, but a clanging bell interrupted him, accompanied by a bellow of, "Lights out!" Henry quickly typed a simple:

I'm doing OK. Miss you. Love you too.

Not long after, their door swung open. Henry recognized one of the boys from the prefects' table, a tablet in his hand.

"Mint?"

"Here," said Murray.

"Wettie?" asked the boy, tapping the screen.

It took Henry a moment to realize the boy meant him. "Here," he whispered.

"Lights out in ten."

"That's Fletcher. He and Fraser are like this," explained Murray, gesturing with two fingers close together once the prefect had moved on.

Henry climbed into his bed and curled up in a ball, staring at the hole in the plaster that looked like a map of France. His sheets felt stiff and unfamiliar. Underneath he could smell his mattress, like a damp dog.

Later, as he lay in the gloom, trying to escape into sleep, Henry felt a strange rumble coming from below. The windows rattled and his bed trembled. He sat up, heart thudding. Then, as quickly as it had started, it was over.

"Did you feel that?" Henry whispered. But the snores coming from Murray's bed told him his room-mate hadn't. Henry shut his eyes and wished he was at home.

The next morning, Tadpole woke late. She scurried down the main tunnel, sidestepping piles of dirt and rock, and the tunnel workers busy with shovels and buckets clearing it up.

"What's all this?" Tadpole asked when she passed by Rockface *(she who chisels stone)*.

"More earth trembles last night – didn't you feel them?"

"I was fast asleep."

Rockface laughed as she went back to shovelling. "Wish I could sleep as soundly as you."

At the school hall, Tadpole was relieved to see everything still as she'd left it. She hurried behind the sheet stretched across the stage and gave the row of firefly lanterns a little shake. The insects woke up and began to glow brighter, casting a warm glow on the cloth.

As Rainbow *(she bright and beaming)* led the fledglings

into the cavern, Tadpole checked her shadow puppets to see the characters were ready for their entrance: Rattlesnake the villain, with his narrow eyes and long tongue. His sidekick, Shadyside, graceless and dim. The hero of the piece, Limelight, carrying her mighty staff. Tadpole was particularly pleased with the character of the wolf. It had taken her ages to cut him out of bark, his mouth bristling with jagged teeth.

She peeked out from behind the cloth. The fledglings were sitting in rows, the fuzz on their faces just beginning to sprout, their chatter, like that of sparrows, filling the cavern. But there was no sign of Shipshape and Waterworks.

Rainbow poked her head round the sheet. "I think we may need to make a start, Tadpole. The crowd's getting restless."

"OK." Tadpole took a deep breath, picked up her drum and began to beat out a steady rhythm. As the drumming got louder, the babbling of the young Greybeards died down.

"Welcome, fledglings," Tadpole called out from her hiding place behind the sheet. "Behold, the story of Limelight and the Wolf." She gave a last flourish on the drum, then moved the scenery into place. A shadow forest appeared on the cloth, the silhouettes of the trees dark and deep. She flipped another cut-out and a pinnacle rose up.

Tadpole took the sticks holding up the Limelight puppet and moved her across the light of the firefly lanterns: on the cloth, the hero came down from the mountain, her shadow dancing along the slope. Tadpole grinned as the fledglings gasped. She had them hooked.

"Many moons ago," she began, "there lived a proud Greybeard called Limelight…"

★

As Rainbow and the cave of fledglings gave her warm applause Tadpole came out from behind her sheet, her legs stiff from crouching, and took a bow.

"That was lovely, Tadpole, thank you," said Rainbow.

"It sounded as if they were enjoying it."

"They always like your plays," said Rainbow. "Now I'd better get them back to class. Though focusing on their sums after such a fun performance might be a problem!"

As the class of fledglings filed out into the corridor, Tadpole scanned the gloom of the cavern and saw Shipshape and Waterworks sitting at the back.

"You came!" She rushed over. "I didn't see you at first."

"We got here just as you started drumming." Shipshape stood up and gave her a hug.

"Great show!" said Waterworks.

"Yes, I really liked the way you made the bear chase

Shadyside." Shipshape pointed at the puppet in Tadpole's hand.

"It was a wolf," said Waterworks.

Shipshape squinted. "Of course, it's a wolf – that's what I meant," she stammered, getting to her feet.

"Well, as fun as that was, I'd better get back to work," said Waterworks.

"That makes two of us. Now where did I put those slates?" Shipshape ran her hand along the bench.

"They're right here, Mum," Tadpole frowned, handing them to her.

"All set?" asked Waterworks.

"I'll be down at Shadowspring to help soon," said Tadpole. She went backstage to pack up her puppets, reaching for her pendant.

"*Great show.*" Snowdrift appeared at her side. "*One of your better ones.*"

"Thanks," said Tadpole.

She carefully took down the sheet and put it into a carry sack with the puppets. Tossing the sack over her shoulder, she left the hall to drop it off at the family den. But, as Tadpole went past the wormery, she saw Slapstick and Tagalong kneeling on the loose earth, drumming their fingers on the surface.

"Hey, Tadpole. What are you up to?" asked Slapstick.

"Heading down to the waterhole. Got to help Dad."

"Nah. You should give us a hand in here," said Tagalong.

Tadpole sighed. "Believe me, I'd love to."

"You should see the size of some of them." Slapstick grabbed hold of a tail and pulled out a giant night crawler. He looked round to see there weren't any elders about and slurped down the writhing creature.

Tadpole thought for a moment. Shadowspring could wait. She scampered in and put down her carry sack. "Maybe I could just taste one or two."

Tagalong handed her a worm. "That's the Tadpole I know."

★

When the bell rang early on Monday morning, Henry woke with a shock. At first, he thought he was back in bed at home, but a quick glance around revealed dingy walls, cobwebs in the corners and a room-mate snoring on the other side of the room. He sat up and pulled back a corner of the curtain. Morning sun flooded the countryside. He'd made it through the first long night. Henry rolled out of bed and opened his cupboard with a squeaking of hinges.

"No one gets up on the first bell," Murray moaned from under his covers.

"Did you feel that tremor last night?"

"What tremor?" Murray grunted. "Go back to bed – there's another bell in twenty minutes."

★

Henry's first class of the day was history, which, he found out, was taught by the headmaster himself. Mr Dossit hurried in late, and began connecting his computer. "Now where's ... ah ... our new boy, Henry Wetwood?"

Henry put his hand up. "Here, sir," he mumbled as he felt all eyes turn to him.

"Good to have you ... ah ... at Halbrook."

"Thank you, sir."

"Looking forward to the school tramp?"

"Tramp?"

"Didn't the others tell you?" Mr Dossit tutted. His moustache wiggled. "To the cairn on Ben Bell. You've arrived just in time. He's in for ... ah ... a treat, isn't he, boys?"

"Yes, Mr Dossit," said the boys.

"The Ben Bell tramp is one of the highlights of the term." Mr Dossit's eyes sparkled.

"Yes, sir," said Henry.

"Will we see a Greybeard this time, sir?" a voice cried out from the back.

The headmaster's moustache waggled again. "Ah ... our mysterious grey friends."

"I hope we do, sir."

"I very much doubt it, Chaudhry," said Mr Dossit. "As much as I'd like to believe they roam these hills, I fear the Greybeards are no more than a collection of stories."

"What stories, sir?"

Mr Dossit fiddled with his laptop. "Well, you know the earliest sighting on these ranges took place in the mid-1700s? A shepherd was out with his lambs … on the northern slopes of Ben Bell as it happens. This man claimed he saw a figure … nine metres high." Mr Dossit chuckled. "But it was later decided to be nothing but a Brocken spectre."

"Brocken spectre?" asked a boy.

The headmaster went over to the whiteboard and found a marker. He started to draw a mountainside, a stick figure and a sun, talking as he scribbled. "The shepherd was … ah … up the hill… Here, yes? And the sun was low like this." Mr Dossit drew beams from the sun to the stick figure. "The light from the sun hit the man and cast a shadow on the mist … making it seem like there was a large figure behind him. An illusion." Mr Dossit completed his diagram.

"But there have been other sightings, haven't there, sir?" said Bony. "Not just these broken specks."

"Of course," said Mr Dossit. He opened his mouth, but then paused and wagged a finger at the class. "Almost had me there again, didn't you, boys? Going off on my pet subject."

There were a few chuckles. The headmaster smoothed his moustache and wiped the board clean. He turned on the overhead projector, waiting while a large map of Europe emerged on the screen. The class groaned.

"Now I know we're all excited about the tramp and our local folklore, but who can tell me what they've learned about … Roman expansion into Britain?" There wasn't a sound in the room. "Who did the reading I assigned on Friday? Did anyone begin drafting their maps?"

There was a shuffling of papers, a cough, but again silence. One or two of the boys opened their tablets and pretended to check.

"The reading is important." The headmaster stood still, his hands clenching and unclenching.

Henry lowered his gaze to the graffiti scraped into the wooden desk top: *Halbrook Smells* catching his eye. He wanted to climb under the desk and hide; he couldn't bear the awkwardness of silence.

"Wetwood!" Mr Dossit called out. "What have you been taught about the spread of the Roman Empire into Britain?"

Henry felt his face flush. He scrambled to remember what he knew. "Wasn't it under Emperor Claudius, sir?" he said at last.

Mr Dossit beamed. "Quite right. Good lad! Beginning in AD 43, Claudius succeeded where … ah … Julius Caesar failed. Now, if we look at this next frame, it shows the gradual growth…"

"Try-hard," someone whispered from the back.

For the rest of the period, Henry kept his head down and worked on his map, drawing tidy boundaries round his countries, placing careful dots for cities, representing mountains and bodies of water – making a key.

"Nice," said Murray, looking over Henry's shoulder at the end of the lesson.

"Thanks."

"You should come to drawing group with me this afternoon."

"Sure." Henry followed his room-mate into the bustle of the corridor, checking his timetable. "I've got gym now – which way is that?" he called out as Murray jostled his way along the hall.

"Down the main staircase and out to the grounds at the back. Big building. Can't miss it!" Murray called back.

Henry checked he had his PE gear in his backpack and scurried down the hall in the opposite direction. "Main staircase, out the back. Big building," he said to himself.

But, emerging into the rear quad of Halbrook Hall, Henry found himself staring at several big buildings he hadn't seen before. He settled on the building that looked most gym-like, chasing after some of the boys he thought he recognized from history class, but discovered it was the science department. Henry spun round, suddenly aware that there were no blazers and backpacks left in the quad. To his right was scaffolding and high metal fencing. A sign on it said **Hazel Halbrook English Department**. A group of men wearing hard hats entered the building site, carrying plasterboard.

Then, over in the corner of the grounds, across a grassy paddock, Henry saw a big building with a red pitched roof and enormous sliding doors. Without any windows, it looked like a giant shed, maybe a small aeroplane hangar – it could certainly fit a whole basketball court inside. Henry ran over.

The door on the side of the building was locked. Henry was about to pull at the bigger sliding door when he stopped. Loud noises came from inside, but not the sound of a teacher's whistle or boys running around – more of a clanking and a rattling. Henry put his ear against the corrugated metal. He could hear the whirr of machinery.

All at once, a loud moan came from inside the shed and the walls began to quiver. Tremors reached up through his shoes. Then the rumbling stopped. Was this the same thing he'd felt in the night? The sliding door started to scrape open and Henry quickly moved down the side of the huge shed. A lorry grumbled through the opening and tore off down the drive, JARVIS AND MACNEIL LTD painted on the side.

Before he could peek inside, the shed door began to close, dragged by another hard-hatted man. He spotted Henry and jerked his head back towards Halbrook. "School's that way. Clear off."

"Sorry, I was trying to find the gym," Henry stammered.

"Do I look like a teacher?" muttered the man, stepping inside and pulling the door shut.

5

Another spell of shuddering in the ground brought the
worm-catching to an end, and Tadpole hurried out of the
wormery and back to the den, cramming the last bit of
night-crawler tail into her mouth. Dumping her props,
she ran down the main tunnel to the lifts, past the quarry
where the miner yeti carved out rock into blocks, and the
hatchery where workers scattered fish food over the small
tank. Tadpole stopped for a moment to watch the top of
the water froth as the fish went into a frenzy.

She chose one of the hollowed-out tree-trunk lifts, each
big enough for a Greybeard, stepped inside and untied the
rope. Far below, the counterweight began its long journey
upwards. With a jerk, the tree trunk began to descend,
taking Tadpole down the darkened shaft until the lift
rested on the ground with a bump.

Shadowspring was busy, lit up by the soft light of

firefly lanterns, a crew of yeti milling about, yodelling to themselves as they worked. Tadpole knew she ought to care more about what went on down here, the important work the Greybeards did, but frankly water-cleaning was boring.

For one thing, it was slow. From start to finish, the whole thing was so *s-l-o-w*. Watching water dribble down through the rock ceiling and land in the barrels just a trickle at a time, the *plop-plop-plop* of the drips enough to drive anyone mad. Then the water going back to the top and being filtered down through wooden chambers of crushed-up stone, shaker yeti pushing and pulling the frames from side to side to remove all the human grime that drained into the ground. More drops into another pool, then more gravel chambers and more shaking and more pools before being scooped up and carried back to the top in buckets to do the same all over again. Then, only when it had been around and around and around, was it ready to go into the waterhole, and out into the world to feed the valley.

And one day Tadpole was meant to oversee all of it – the whole sett.

She spotted Shipshape and Waterworks over by the giant filter, inspecting the shaker boxes with Rainstorm, and ran to join them.

"Ah, there you are at last." Shipshape gestured at the large sand timer on the wall. "What took you so long?"

"Sorry. It was harder to pack up than I thought." Tadpole saw the Guardian raise his eyebrows. "Did you feel those trembles just now?"

"They seem to be becoming more frequent," Rainstorm complained.

"Well, we were just about to begin measuring," said Waterworks as they made their way to the edge of the giant pool. He took a knotted rope from where it hung on a peg and handed it to Tadpole. "You remember how to do it, right?"

"Yep." Tadpole dangled the weighted rope over the surface of the water and slowly played it out, counting the knots as she went. "Five," she called out. "Ten … fifteen … seventeen." Tadpole stopped. The weight was on the bottom.

"Seventeen?" asked Waterworks.

Tadpole jerked on the line, feeling the weight rise off the bottom, and let it drift down to settle again. She gathered the rope back up, counting the knots. "Seventeen," she confirmed.

Waterworks let out a long breath as he jotted the figures down. "That's two knots lower than just yestermoon."

"A drop of two knots? In one moon?" Shipshape squinted at the figures on the slate.

"And the water is already much lower than it should be this time of cycle."

"Most worrying," muttered Rainstorm. "Any idea why it's lower?"

"I'm afraid not." Waterworks twirled his moustache.

"Very strange indeed." Shipshape shuffled over to the edge of the pool and peered down at the water. She took a couple of steps closer to get a better look.

"Mum!" cried Tadpole. But she was too late.

Shipshape stepped into thin air and fell, plummeting into the waterhole. She hit the water with a thump.

"Sweet whiskers!" gasped Waterworks, dropping to his knees at the edge. "Don't worry, we'll get you out!"

Without hesitating, Rainstorm took the rope from Tadpole's hands. He wrapped one end of it round his back and threw the other down into the water. "Grab hold!" he yelled.

Tadpole watched as Shipshape floundered, treading water, desperately searching for it. "To your right!" she yelled down.

"Got it," spluttered Shipshape, grasping the measuring rope.

"Take hold!" Rainstorm commanded and Waterworks and Tadpole grabbed the rope. Crewcut *(she with short head hair)* and some of the others clambered down from their stations, and ran over to join them. Hand over hand they heaved, pulling Shipshape over the lip of the waterhole to safety.

Dad and Tadpole kneeled beside her. "Are you all right, Mum?" asked Tadpole.

Water streamed from the silverback's fur. "I-I think so," she panted. Waterworks helped her to her feet.

Rainstorm cupped his hands and called out to the vast cavern. "All stop! All stop!" The sound of shaking boxes and pouring water died down.

"Take a short break, Greybeards," said Waterworks to Crewcut and the others.

"That was quick thinking, Rainstorm, thank you," said Shipshape when she got her breath back. She slipped the sash off her shoulders and wrung the spider silk out. Rainstorm bowed.

"What happened?" asked Waterworks.

"I must have slipped, that's all," said Shipshape, embarrassed. "And I've made the whole water plant grind to a halt. Foolish Greybeard. I'm so sorry."

Tadpole stared at her, puzzled. "Mum, you stepped right off the edge."

"Are you sure everything's OK?" Waterworks added.

"Everything's fine!" Shipshape snorted. She put the sash back on and smoothed it out, then let out a long breath. "I've just got a lot on my mind, that's all. I slipped. Sorry."

"Not to worry." Waterworks peered down at the waterhole. "We'll have to follow the accident procedure, run the fine filter through the water, but we'll be back up to speed by the end of the moon."

"Thanks," said Shipshape. "Now we'd better go and check on the lodgings for the ambassadors, Rainstorm." She gave Waterworks a nuzzle and headed for the lifts.

Rainstorm paused for a moment, looking at the edge of the water chamber and then at Shipshape, before running to catch up with her.

Tadpole saw a look of unease cross her dad's face as he watched Shipshape climb into the lift. She felt it too.

"*It's like she couldn't see,*" said Snowdrift. "*It's been happening a lot of late.*"

"That's just what I was thinking," said Tadpole under her breath.

Waterworks ran his fingers through his beard. "Come on then, Tadpole, we need to get started."

6

"How was your first day?" asked Murray as they crossed the quad that afternoon. A lorry drove out from the big barn and rumbled past them. Whatever they were doing in there, lorryloads of something were coming out.

"All right, I suppose." Henry told his room-mate about how he was late for PE and had to climb the rope for most of the period. He showed Murray his red, raw hands.

"Sorry, should have given you better directions," said Murray. "I forgot what it's like to be new here."

The art room was hidden in a basement, and drawing club turned out to be a small group, just Murray, Henry and half a dozen other juniors, watched by a tiny teacher perched on a stool beside a blank sketchpad on an easel.

"This is Henry, Ms Williams," said Murray. "I'll show him how to get set up."

"Welcome, Henry. Always good to see a new face." The

teacher beamed. "You'll need some sketching pencils today, boys, and make sure you have a comfortable workspace."

Murray chose a table and they set up their easels.

"Are those your drawings?" asked Henry, pointing at Murray's black portfolio.

Murray opened the folder and rummaged around, handing him a sheaf of papers. Henry flipped through – there were lots of detailed pen-and-ink drawings of cars, a pineapple, a bandit wearing goggles, the name 'Murray' a dozen ways. There were also several landscapes painted in watercolours – Henry recognized the hills that framed the school. The final painting was of a large grey ape peering out from a forest.

"That's one of a Greybeard." Murray sniffed.

"What's with all this Greybeard stuff?" asked Henry. "Does Mr Dossit really believe in them?"

"Oh yes, he's always going on about Greybeards, though no one has seen one in a hundred years," said Murray. "Greybeards are supposed to like coming out in the mist. People hear heavy footsteps behind them, but when they turn around there's nothing there."

Henry looked at the dark shape in Murray's painting. It didn't look friendly. "Imagine meeting one." He handed back the pictures. "These are really good."

"Thanks – my dad thinks art is a waste of time," Murray sighed.

Now Fraser and Fletcher sloped into the art room, looking decidedly uncomfortable.

"Hurry up and find your places, boys. You're late," Ms Williams tutted. "We're drawing partner portraits today." Fraser and Fletcher groaned.

Murray leaned over. "They'd rather be on the football pitch with their mates, but you have to take an art option at some point if you want to finish school. The fact is, they'd both be really good if they gave themselves the chance – just don't dare tell them."

When Ms Williams finished giving them tips about technique, Henry and Murray turned their easels so they faced each other, and Henry began scratching at the paper with his pencil. Watchful, wide eyes, a hint of freckles, cheeks a little bit puffed out. Murray's was a kind face, thought Henry.

★

That evening, coming back late from the shower room (he'd waited so long for a shower that almost all the hot water had run out), Henry saw boys bustling about with backpacks, digging around in cupboards, pulling out walking boots and weatherproof jackets. The second floor was buzzing.

Murray was sitting on top of his own bag, trying to wedge it shut. "Mr Dossit expects a full survival pack, sleeping bag and all. Just so you know. You'd better make sure you have it all." He waved his list at Henry.

"I'll double-check," said Henry, quickly getting into his pyjamas.

He went through the checklist again. Spare socks, plasters, torch – he'd missed off heaps. Good thing Murray had reminded him. Henry was scrabbling through his cupboard to find it all when there was a clang of the bell and the shout of lights out.

Almost immediately, Fraser Ragbone appeared in his dressing gown – velvety and red – a tablet in one hand, a backpack over his shoulder.

"Murray Mint." Fraser tapped the screen. "And Wettie."

"Present," said Henry.

"Glad you're here, Wettie. I meant to catch up with you before." Fraser slipped the backpack off his shoulder and let it hit the floor with a thud. "You need to carry my gear tomorrow."

"Yours?"

Fraser grinned. "Shove all my things in your bag, and I'll come back to collect my empty pack."

"You're joking," said Murray.

"Quiet, Mint." Fraser glared at him. "I don't care if your dad is Dossit's boss."

"Yes, Fraser."

"Now a favour is a favour and you owe me one. Isn't

51

that right, Wettie?" Fraser smirked as he left. "I'll be back in fifteen."

Henry started pressing his own things to the bottom of the backpack with a sigh. "What did he mean, your dad is Mr Dossit's boss?"

Murray let out a long breath. "Dad and his partners and Mr Dossit are working together – something to do with the new building that's going up. Everyone thinks that's the only reason I'm here."

"I'm sure that's not true."

Murray managed a smile. "Thanks. But they think it all the same."

There was another knock on the door. "Mrs Nettles here," the house parent called out. "Make yourselves decent." Henry went to let her in. "Just checking you're ready, Henry," said Mrs Nettles. "First tramp for you."

"Yes, thanks, Mrs Nettles," Henry said. "Just packing the last of my things away now."

"Good to hear. I'll leave you boys to it." She turned and was about to go when she spotted the extra backpack sitting on the floor. She paused. "Why do you have a spare bag in here, boys?"

Murray said nothing.

"Whose rucksack is it?" asked Mrs Nettles. "Well?" When the boys stayed silent, she opened the top of the rucksack and saw the name printed on the inside flap.

"Fraser Ragbone," she read. "And why is his backpack in here?"

Henry just shrugged.

Mrs Nettles went out and called down the corridor. "Mr Ragbone, a word, if you please."

Fraser appeared in the doorway. "Yes, Mrs Nettles?"

"Your backpack. Why is it in these boys' room?"

Fraser looked blank.

"I've heard some seniors – some *misguided* seniors – try to get the juniors to carry their things for them all the way up to Ben Bell. Would you know anything about that?"

"Not me, Mrs Nettles," Fraser smiled. "I was collecting a few things that some of the other boys borrowed from me when I remembered I had to check the roll. I was just leaving the backpack here so I wouldn't have to carry it around. Isn't that right?"

Henry and Murray both nodded.

"Then, if you've finished the roll, you'd best pick it up, hadn't you? Come along."

"Of course, Mrs Nettles." Fraser handed her the tablet. The prefect bent down and shouldered his pack. "Thanks for keeping an eye on it, Henry," he said, following Mrs Nettles out of the room.

"Lights out, boys." Mrs Nettles closed the door behind her.

"I hate to say it, but you're in for it now," said Murray.

7

That night, a glimmer of light in her den woke Tadpole.
She opened her eyes to see Snowdrift standing in her
room, holding a lantern.

I must be dreaming, thought Tadpole.

"Grandfather?"

Snowdrift raised a finger to his lips. *"You need to be
quiet. It's the middle of the night."*

"What are you doing?" Tadpole hissed.

"Listen, I've been thinking." Snowdrift sat down on the
edge of her nest. Tadpole shifted over to make room, the
woven tree boughs creaking under her weight. Snowdrift
toyed with the lichen pillow as he tried to find the right
words. He let out a long breath. *"After what happened in
Shadowspring this morning, I think we have to face facts."*

"Mum's eyes."

Snowdrift nodded. *"There's something wrong."*

"I think so too."

"*I don't need to remind you how important this Gathering is.*"

"I know, Grandfather," said Tadpole.

"*Well, I have an idea to help. But it's a little risky.*"

"OK," said Tadpole slowly.

"*The cure for Shipshape's eyesight is in Hazel's hut.*"

Tadpole gulped. "Hazel's hut? Really?"

"*I've told you about my visits there?*"

Tadpole nodded.

"*Well, in her hut, Hazel had many contraptions. I think one in particular can help.*"

"What contraption?"

"*They're like two pieces of frozen ice. Hazel wore them on her nose.*" Snowdrift pointed to his face. "*They helped her fading eyes to see things clearly.*"

Tadpole considered this. "How do you know?"

"*She told me, of course,*" said Snowdrift. "*Hazel called them* specktakulls. *Before I buried her, I took them off her nose and put them back in her hut.*"

"And they might work for Mum too?"

"*In many things, we Greybeards are wiser than humans, but there's a lot of their learning that is much better than ours, just like these specktakulls. I think they're worth a try.*" Snowdrift pushed himself up. "*I plan to sneak out of the sett and get them.*"

"Peak-running?" Tadpole snorted. "Please."

"There's still some striding left in these legs." Snowdrift patted his knees.

"No, there isn't," said Tadpole. "I hate to keep reminding you, but you don't really exist, remember? Just how do you propose to actually grab hold of the *specktakulls* with hands that aren't real?"

"I could give it a go."

"And just where is Hazel's hut anyway?"

"It's completely hidden. Like a secret," said Snowdrift. *"But I made a map."*

"A map?"

"The one in your hands," said Snowdrift.

Now Tadpole looked down and realized she was clutching Grandfather's pendant. Tadpole loosened the cord and drew it over her head. The front of the pendant was smooth, and getting smoother all the time from her touch, but on the back were some symbols pressed into the clay. Tadpole ran her fingers over the indentations – she'd never paid them much attention. Now she leaned over and gave the firefly lantern a gentle shake.

In the soft glow, Tadpole studied the marks. All this time, she had believed they were part of a pattern – an artist's stamp. Now she could see a peak, a path, the woods and a ring of rocks. And in the middle of the ring of rocks was a pitched roof.

"It still doesn't change the fact you can't get there," she pointed out.

"*That's very true*," agreed Snowdrift. "*It's really a job for the living.*"

Tadpole stared at his shape, a thought on the tip of her tongue. Then she turned away and curled towards the wall, leaving Snowdrift standing there.

"Goodnight, Grandfather," she whispered, closing her eyes.

★

Deep underground, in the depths of the Himalayas, Dahl *(he who smells the fiercest)* and Jiffi *(she always in a hurry)* of the Mountain Yeti stood hand in hand on the bank of the waterway, watching Tick and the others do a final check of the canoe in the dim light of the glow-worms.

Jiffi gave a little giggle. She took Dahl's hand and placed it on her large belly. "He's lively today – feel him kick."

"No, *she's* lively." Dahl gave her a nuzzle. "Just like her mother."

"Awkward," groaned Tick *(he with no time to waste)*.

"Aw, it's sweet," whispered Plumm *(she sweet on the outside with hard centre)*.

At the back of the canoe, Nagg *(he who pesters)* sat perched on his cushion, a bark map of the waterways resting on his lap. "Now are you absolutely sure you have the fungus, Tick?"

"Yes, Nagg." Tick pointed to the earthenware jars in the centre of the canoe.

"Both kinds?"

"Yes, Nagg."

Nagg patted the sling hanging over his chest. "And I have the etching of the greeting to the Collective from our Council of Elders. We may therefore depart. Paddles ready."

The yeti took hold of the oars while Dahl bent down to loosen the rope looped round a stalagmite.

"Now you will look after yourselves," said Jiffi.

"Don't worry, Mum. We've done this before," said Tick.

"I know you have."

"Just think, when we get back, you'll have a new fledgling in the family," said Plumm.

"*A journey of a thousand strides begins with a single step.*" Dahl touched his hand to his chest and then to his head.

"*Fine words butter no parsnips,*" Nagg replied, returning the farewell. "I expect a fast stroke, younglings."

"Yes, Nagg," said Plumm as Dahl gave the canoe a gentle shove away from the bank and into the current. She leaned forwards and murmured in Tick's ear, "Sweet fungus, give me strength. I hope he's not like this all the way to the Greybeards."

"Don't even start," whispered Tick.

To begin with, when the Council of Elders chose him and Plumm to represent the Mountain Yeti at the Gathering, they were thrilled. But, when they'd learned that Nagg was the elder leading their delegation, they'd been less than overjoyed.

They needed the Gathering to go well. So much was at stake. The first meeting of the Collective in living memory. At a time when many parts of the Earth and its creatures faced grave danger, yeti and people needed to come together – it was their only chance of survival. Tick just hoped that some of the others felt the same way. But Nagg was always quick to share his feelings about humans, and they weren't kind.

★

Jowll *(she with big jaw)* of the Amomongo staggered through the rainforest, doing her best not to drop an enormous beehive wrapped in cloth.

"Steady, steady," said Croakk *(he with hoarse voice)*. With his face pressed up against the side of the hive, he could feel the bees buzzing angrily inside.

"They still want to know just why they're going to the lands to the north at all," Jowll puffed.

"We've been through all that." Croakk raised his voice

so the bees might hear him through the cloth. "They need more pollinators up there."

"Don't worry, you'll love it," said Jowll.

"We'll have you settled in a moment," rasped Croakk.

★

"Now are you sure you know where we're going?" said Strut of the Orang Pendek *(he with bouncing walk)*. He wound his long hair into a bun and secured it with a twig. "I'm not getting in that boat until you promise me." He sat down on the bridge of rock spanning the waterway to make his point.

"No need to get your hair in a twist. We just have to take the passage north, following the map." Mould *(he with odd growth)* put down the enormous bunch of spiky fruit he was carrying and got the map out of his basket. Unfurling it, he tapped at a snaking line. The small yeti paused for a moment. "The big 'N' means north, right?"

★

In the wetlands of the Bigfoot, Posterior *(he with wide behind)* pushed through a thicket, a large satchel on his back. He dropped it into the boat. "That's the last of the supplies. The farewell committee is right behind me."

Victor *(he who always wins)* sat bobbing in the front of their dugout canoe, peering down into the clear waters.

A manatee glided beneath the boat with lazy wafts of her tail, then floated to the surface, poking her nostrils above the water. With a gentle breath, she sank back down to the sand on the bottom. "Look after the place until we get back, Sirenia," Victor called down into the water, gripping the sides of the canoe as Posterior climbed on board.

Moments later, the Bigfoot Council appeared on the shore, their fur as pale as the wisps of moss dangling from the trees, prodding the uneven ground with their staffs. The yeti formed a line on the bank of the spring.

Orator the silverback *(she who speaks well in public)* handed down a parchment. "Our cry for help, Victor."

"Carry it safely for our sake and for the manatees'," said Camphor *(he whose smell clears the nostrils)*.

Victor bowed. "We will."

As Posterior and Victor pushed off from the bank and drifted along the narrow channel, the elders began to croon a song of farewell, their hands raised in salute, while a paddle-like tail appeared above the water and waved, spurring them on.

8

On the morning of the tramp, the boys filed into the
dining hall to pick up their packed lunches: a round of
sandwiches, a piece of fruit and a couple of biscuits. Each
boy also got a shiny bottle of Pure Origins water. Henry
grabbed the food and began to leave.

"Don't you want your water?" asked the cook.

"No thanks, I already have a flask," said Henry.

"Fair enough."

Seeing all the bottles sitting there with their blue lids
made Henry think back to the beach last summer.

★

It had been a scorcher of a day. After a quick dip in
the sea, Henry left his parents on their beach towels to
investigate the rocks. He clambered up the jagged stone
in his flip-flops and jumped over a narrow channel on

to another larger outcrop, which immediately became 'Henryland'.

The best bit about Henryland – other than the fact that he had the little island to himself – was the rock pool. Henry sat down on the edge of the clear water and admired the tiny hermit crabs ambling along on the sandy bottom; the translucent shrimp darting between seaweed.

Then, clambering round the rock to explore the far side of the pool, Henry saw it: a flash of bright blue on the bottom. At first, he thought maybe it was an exotic fish, some rare sea creature. But then, looking closer, Henry saw it was a bottle-top – the kind that came with water bottles. Someone's rubbish. Henry reached in and fished the bottle-top out. Then it moved in his palm.

Henry yelped and dropped it back down, eyeing it suspiciously. After a time, claws edged out of the plastic, followed by a tiny face. It was a hermit crab. The bottle-top its home – its shell.

Henry took it out again, and sure enough, tucked in the back of the bottle lid, was the crab. Henry felt a little queasy. It seemed so wrong. There was a part of him that wanted to gently pull the poor creature out, so that it could find a new home – a proper, natural shell, not a piece of rubbish. But would he hurt it? Henry lowered the bottle-top crab back into the water.

On his way back to his parents, Henry now realized that the bins on the beach were all overflowing with plastic bottles, disposable coffee cups and food wrappers.

"Find anything interesting?" asked his mum, handing him a towel from the bag.

Henry told them about the rock pool, the hermit crab and the plastic.

"Awful," grumbled his dad. "Whose rubbish ends up there?"

As Henry dried himself off, he caught a glimpse inside their own cool bag with its throwaway water bottles and packaged meals. *I have a fairly good idea*, he thought.

★

With their lunches packed away, the boys trudged out to meet the headmaster on the steps of Halbrook Hall, dressed in full tramping gear. Mr Dossit clapped his hands for attention. When the assembled boys carried on murmuring, Mr Dossit clapped again. He rapped his walking stick on the stone steps. Finally Mrs Nettles bellowed out, "Quiet, everyone!" and the school grudgingly fell silent.

The headmaster cleared his throat. "Now I hope you're all … ah … ready for our ascent today. Full survival packs, yes?"

"Yes, Mr Dossit," answered a hundred voices.

"All been checked by the prefects, sir," Fraser Ragbone called out from the crowd.

"Well done, Ragbone. The forecast promises a fine, cloudless day for our climb. But, all the same, we walk in pairs and … ah … keep your eyes on the tramper ahead."

"Yes, Mr Dossit."

"Enjoy the walk! You'll be having your sandwiches on the summit of Ben Bell before you know it – that is, of course, if the Greybeards don't … ah … have something else planned!" Mr Dossit chortled. A few of the teachers smiled, but the boys stayed silent. "Right, off we go! Mrs Nettles, you take the rear, please. I'll lead."

★

That morning, Tadpole stumbled out of her nest and into the living den to join her mum and dad, her hair wild and fuzzy. She'd tossed and fidgeted in her nest, thinking about what Snowdrift had told her.

"Morning, sleepybeard," said Shipshape. "There's a pot of nettle tea if you want some."

"Thanks," Tadpole murmured, grabbing a cup.

"So what's on the agenda for today?" asked Waterworks.

Tadpole shrugged. "Not sure. Might catch up with my friends."

"I've got lots on," Shipshape sighed. "Meetings. Inspections. On top of everything, Rainstorm has come up with a plan to send out guard patrols. With the Collective coming, he's worried about the number of humans out on the ranges."

"Patrols, really?"

"We're going to discuss it at Council. But there's still so much else to do."

"You'll get there," said Waterworks.

There was a rap on the door. Tadpole got up to answer it.

Rainstorm stood in the tunnel with his cousin Hindsight *(she who looks backwards)* beside him, her wiry whiskers reaching down to her chest. Hindsight carried a scroll in her hands. "Good morning."

"Morning." Tadpole ushered them in.

"*A toad on the breakfast bench is worth two in the pond.*" Rainstorm touched his hand to his head.

"*If you go to a donkey's house, don't talk about her ears,*" replied Waterworks.

"I haven't had a chance to look at your ideas yet." Shipshape gestured at the pile of slates sitting on the table. "Let me just put on my sash." She looked around the room, eyes narrowed.

Rainstorm glanced over at Hindsight. He cleared his throat. "Actually, we come here on a different matter."

"Oh?" Shipshape paused.

Rainstorm smoothed back the hair on his head.

He opened his mouth, coughed, then fell silent. He tried again, but still said nothing.

"Say what you need to say, Rainstorm." Shipshape gestured at one of the chairs.

"Perhaps we could discuss it in private?" Rainstorm sat down, shifting uneasily.

"Of course. Tadpole, please leave us for a moment."

Tadpole gave them a nod and left, drawing the moss curtain behind her. She thought about going back to her room, but then stopped and pressed herself against the wall, peeking through a tiny gap.

Rainstorm leaned forwards, resting his hands on his staff. "Yestermoon at the waterhole…"

"An accident," said Shipshape. "Don't worry. I'm fine."

Rainstorm sighed. "That's just it, I don't think you are." Tadpole could see the Guardian squirming. "Your eyesight, Shipshape. It grows worse."

There was silence in the room. Tadpole felt cold. Finally Shipshape spoke. "What in sweet whiskers do you mean?"

"It hasn't escaped my attention these many moons. We've seen you at Council meetings squinting at slates, trying to read the writing … trouble recognizing faces… The other moon you couldn't tell it was Tadpole in the slopping trench."

"She was covered in mud," Shipshape protested.

"It was her, as plain as anything."

"Please."

"What about losing things when they're right in front of you?" asked Rainstorm. He leaned over and lifted the Stinking Sash from where it lay on the back of a nearby chair, handing it to her.

Shipshape took the sash from him, jaw clenched. "Nonsense," she said quietly.

Rainstorm threw up his hands. "Shipshape, you fell into the waterhole! We were all there! You didn't see you were at the edge and stepped right off."

"Can you believe this?" Shipshape turned to Waterworks.

Waterworks was silent. When he finally spoke, his voice was a whisper. "My love, your eyes…" He paused, unable to continue.

"There can be no more denying it, Shipshape," said Rainstorm.

The room went still. Tadpole pressed her head hard against the rock wall, hardly able to bear any more.

At last, Shipshape let out a long breath. "I told myself it wasn't happening… The headaches, the blurred vision. Tried to keep it hidden, hoping it would get better. I can still see, but it's just all a bit…"

Waterworks reached for her hand. He sniffed and wiped his eyes. "You should have said."

"I didn't want to worry you and Tadpole," said

Shipshape. "I even went to see Peppermint for an examination."

"And?" asked Hindsight.

"She gave me a big dose of leeches, but they didn't do any good."

Peppermint the apothecary *(she who soothes)* was always dishing out leeches, thought Tadpole.

There was a long silence.

"So what now?" Shipshape asked.

"It pains me to say it, but as Guardian it is my duty." Rainstorm coughed again. "You must relinquish the sash."

"What!" Waterworks spluttered.

"But the Gathering is almost here," said Shipshape.

Now Hindsight broke in. "The slab laws are quite clear on this." She unrolled the parchment. "*If a silverback should suffer an ailment or injury that hinders them from doing their duties to the best of their abilit—*"

"But I'm still capable!" said Shipshape. "I can get by with things the way they are. I have no intention of stepping aside."

"Please see sense," said Rainstorm. "You could have been seriously hurt. We had to shut down water production for most of the moon! How long before you run into a human out on the peaks without seeing them? Or worse, Shipshape?"

"I will not hand over the sash, Guardian."

Rainstorm pushed himself back in his chair. He lowered his head. "Then you leave me no choice. There must be a challenge."

"A challenge?"

"A formal contest for silverback. For the good of the sett."

"But we work so well together, Rainstorm. Have I not treated you fairly as my second in command?"

"This is not personal, Shipshape. With the Collective upon us, we just can't afford to make mistakes. It's bad enough that the water level in Shadowspring drops moon by moon."

Now Waterworks spoke up. "But the sash is handed down from parent to oldest child – everyone knows that. Tadpole is next in line."

"Yes, that is true," admitted Rainstorm. "Dare I say it, while the youngling has many fine, er … *qualities*, the sett must have someone it can depend on right now. Someone they can trust. Tadpole would rather play with mud and puppets."

Tadpole felt her face burning.

"Again the laws are quite clear," said Hindsight. "*If the Guardian deems it necessary for the good of the sett, they may lawfully challenge the silverback for the right to wear the Stinking Sash. The challenger may determine the time, the place and the contest…*"

"But no one has challenged for the sash in living memory," said Waterworks. "That law hasn't been called upon for many generations."

"It is still our law," said Hindsight.

"Don't do this, Rainstorm," said Shipshape.

"For the good of the sett, the contest needs to happen swiftly," said the Guardian. "This very moon."

"And the type of challenge you've chosen?" Waterworks demanded.

"Yettiwinks."

"I see," said Shipshape.

"You may not believe it, but it was never my intention to do this to you," said Rainstorm.

"Apology not accepted," Waterworks grumbled.

"So be it."

Tadpole heard the Guardian get to his feet. She tiptoed to her room in a hurry and sat on her nest with a thump, her heart pounding.

Tadpole reached for her necklace and Snowdrift materialized next to her.

"*The smell of blood always draws the shark,*" he muttered.

"It's not fair," grumbled Tadpole. "He knows you need good aim for yettiwinks."

"*Precisely why he chose it.*"

"Now we really need those *specktakulls*," said Tadpole.

"*We've been through that.*"

"I know – I've been thinking about it all night. I need to be the one to go." Tadpole lifted the pendant and tapped the map. "I could be there and back before anyone knows I've gone."

Snowdrift shook his head. "*But the danger. What if you were caught? If Rainstorm or the others were to find out…*"

"You don't need to remind me. I'll be careful."

"*A fine sort of grandfather I am, letting my grandfluff do such a thing.*"

"I'll be super careful," Tadpole insisted. "And you're the best kind of grandfather."

Snowdrift thought for a moment. "*No one else must know, Tadpole. Not even your parents. For their sake, it's best they are kept in the dark. Tell them and the gatekeeper you're going out foraging.*"

"Got it."

Tadpole looked up as Shipshape poked her head in the doorway. "Were you saying something, Tadpole?"

"No, but I heard Rainstorm, Mum. I'm so sorry."

"That makes two of us."

"How *are* your eyes?"

"I'd rather not talk about it." Shipshape sat down on the bed. "But I could certainly use a hug."

Tadpole wrapped her arms round her mum. "I've got that covered."

9

The line of boys clambered over a stile in the fence and left the school grounds. Following the trail into the forest, they forded a narrow stream, and started to climb. To begin with, the track that wound its way to the summit of Ben Bell was gentle and even underfoot, and wide enough for two people to walk side by side. Even so, the stiff straps of Henry's backpack dug into his shoulders and his thighs burned. Waiting for Murray to go to the loo behind a shrub, their little group fell quite far behind. Mrs Nettles, in her khaki shorts, had pushed on ahead, arms pumping, setting the pace.

Henry panted as he tried to keep up with the others. He stopped to take a swig from his flask. Now that they were above the treeline, short brown scrub and clumps of pale purple flowers covered the slopes, giving way to bare rock. To his right, a pair of rounded boulders like gigantic marbles thrust their way out of the earth.

Hardly the kind of terrain these Greybeards could possibly hide in. Henry chuckled at himself. What was he thinking? Greybeards were just a story. Looking up ahead, he noticed that Murray and the others had pushed on without stopping for him, and ran to catch up.

★

Tadpole waited until Shipshape and Waterworks were busy practising yettiwinks in the living den, then she slung her carry sack over her shoulder and felt for the pendant around her neck.

"*Are you sure you're up for this?*" said Snowdrift.

"Yes."

"*Remember – two pieces of ice joined together.*"

"I'll find them."

"*And Grandfluff, above all, be careful. If there's the smallest whiff of danger, come straight back.*"

Tadpole left the den and padded up to the main tunnel, the corridors already filled with Greybeards stopping to spread the news.

"He's bound to win."

"Rainstorm has picked his moment well. I hear she can barely see her nose in front of her face."

"I thought something wasn't quite right with her – didn't I say?"

"There hasn't been a challenge like this for yonks."

"Shipshape has done a whiffling job leading us – no complaints there from me."

"At least, if Rainstorm does win, it means that wayward youngling won't wear the sash one day. That's something."

"Didn't take long for the news to travel," muttered Tadpole. The whispers died away as she ran past, the Greybeards staring at their feet. *Wayward youngling*, thought Tadpole. *That truly is how everyone sees me.*

At the sett entrance, Tadpole ran into Deadend *(he who blocks the way)*. The gatekeeper saw the bag over Tadpole's shoulder. "Collecting, is it?"

Tadpole looked at her feet. "Reindeer droppings. For Mum."

Deadend cocked his giant head to one side and then the other. He scratched his whiskers. "OK," he said at last. "But you need to keep your wits about you – use the mist when it comes. There have been more humans than usual around and I'm not happy about it. Avoid the human path to the north, understand? Not so much as a whisper."

"Yes, Deadend."

The gatekeeper gestured to Toothpick *(she tall and thin)* and Nutcracker *(he with fearsome grip)*, the sett guards. They took hold of the rope and heaved, hand over hand. The slab was raised to reveal a darkened crevice. Tadpole smiled at the guards and ducked through, clambering along the rocky floor towards the growing light. She heard the gate shut behind her.

At last, at the surface, Tadpole lifted her head and sniffed the breeze, nostrils widening, eyes closed. Nothing. Tadpole took another breath, deeper this time, drawing in the thick mist until her chest swelled. She caught rich pinewood and heath; the odour of wildcat – there was a litter tucked away somewhere nearby; and a spicy pile of reindeer droppings – she'd grab those on the way back in.

Hazel's hut – was she really going there? What if someone saw her? Tadpole pushed the idea out of her head. Her mum needed her.

Tadpole listened for the tell-tale sound of stomping human feet, for their loud prattle, but again there was nothing. Confident that she was alone, Tadpole was about to climb out from behind the rocks when she heard footsteps in the scrub and dropped down.

A mountain hare bounded up the hillside through the mist, his long limbs a blur. The hare came to a stop and stood tall at her feet, chest proud. The hare's coat was still dusky-brown, though with winter on the horizon Tadpole knew it would gradually change to white over the coming moons, until the creature was almost impossible to find in the snow.

"You gave me a start, Lepus." Tadpole leaned over and rubbed the soft down between the hare's ears and round the nape of his neck the way she knew her companion liked.

"You off collecting?" Lepus chirruped.

Tadpole looked back down the crevice. "Something else. It's a bit tricky," she whispered. "I'm searching for a human hut in the woods."

Lepus's ears twitched. "A human hut? Really? Where?"

Tadpole loosened the cord from around her neck and showed the hare her pendant. "Snowdrift made me a map."

"I'd better come to watch your back."

Tadpole smiled, glad that he had offered. "That would be great."

"Need to be careful, though. Plenty of humans about north of here."

"I've been warned. You ready to run?" Tadpole steadied her nerves and stood up. A last check to see that the mountainside was empty, then she began to stride downhill through the scrub. The yeti's arms swung low by her sides, the soles of her feet seeking out the smooth patches of stone on the hillside, pausing by Wildcat Rock for a moment to crouch down, allowing her short grey fur to blend in with the stone – checking the symbols on the pendant, before carrying on, peak-running as Greybeards had done since time began.

Striding over the ranges was about the only time Tadpole really felt herself. Sometimes she wished she could peak-run without stopping. Go wherever her feet took her. Somewhere other than stuck in an underground sett, all eyes on her, the daughter of the silverback. How could she possibly measure up to someone like her mother? No one understood just how hard that was.

A few moons ago, Tadpole had overheard her mum and dad talking when they thought she was asleep. When the Gathering was over, a group of Greybeards was going to join another sett on their return voyage. Greybeards hadn't travelled anywhere for as long as anyone could remember so it was time, and Tadpole desperately wanted to go. But she knew the handful of yeti chosen would be elders and not younglings – especially not ones like her. There was no chance she'd ever get to travel like the Mountain Yeti.

But, right now, she had bigger problems.

★

At the top of Ben Bell, Henry admired the ranges spread out before him, the peaks barren and blunt. The wind had a bite to it up here, but underneath all his layers Henry was still sweating. Though his legs and back ached from the climb, he'd made it. He gazed along the length of the winding path, snapping photos with his phone – surprised by how high they'd climbed. Towards the peaks to the north, a lake lay below the slopes, cold and grey. A few of the faraway mountaintops wore a dusting of snow.

The wild mountain ranges were like something right out of the pages of an adventure story. *The Hobbit* maybe, or *Tintin in Tibet*. Tintin climbing high into the mountains to search for his friend – crossing paths with a yeti. Were Greybeards like yeti? Henry wondered. He knew he wasn't as brave as Tintin.

The boys sat in little clusters round the cairn, tucking into their packed lunches. Henry slumped down on a flat boulder near Murray and the others. Fraser caught his eye and gave him a smirk, his mouth full of food, and Henry looked away.

The boys had finished their lunches and were getting restless, throwing stones to see who could launch one furthest down the mountain, when Mr Dossit announced it was time to head back.

Though it had started as a bright day of blue skies, three quarters of the way down the mountain, just when they were approaching the treeline, the sky became overcast, the air cooled and a thick fog descended. Voices became muffled and dim.

"Why am I not surprised?" said Krish, Bony's room-mate. "Always the same on these tramps."

"As long as we can see the person in front, we'll be all right," said Murray.

"If that person knows where they're going," added Bony.

"Mrs Nettles!" Murray shouted. But there was no

response. The line of boys slowed down to a crawl.

Henry kept his eye on Murray's back, and on the stony path. "Hold on a sec." He crouched down to tie his bootlace. But, when he straightened up, he saw that the others hadn't noticed he'd stopped.

"Guys?" Henry called out.

There was no sound but the soft, muted sigh of the wind. The hillside had all but disappeared, and the valley below – and the line between land and sky. All was grey.

As long as you stick to the path, you'll be fine, thought Henry. *In a moment, the others will notice you're not there and stop.*

He stumbled along the path, one step at a time, making sure he could still see the stones on the ground in front of him. It was slow going. Henry glanced round; there was nothing behind him. Then he saw some murky silhouettes ahead.

"Hello?" he squeaked.

10

A tall figure loomed out of the fog. Fraser Ragbone, Fletcher by his side. The boys stopped, hands in pockets.

"Lost, are we, Wettie?" said Fletcher.

"No, I-I was just catching up with Murray and the others." Henry gestured over their shoulders.

"Oh yeah, we passed them," said Fraser. "They were coming back to get you, but we told them we'd find you instead."

"Thanks, but I'll see if I can catch up with them," said Henry and he made to carry on.

But Fraser and Fletcher moved closer together, blocking the path. Henry's head barely reached their shoulders.

"It's very foggy, Wettie," said Fraser. "I think you'd better stay with us."

"Foggy ... Wettie, that's funny," said Fletcher.

Henry looked down at his shoes, his mouth suddenly dry. "I never told Mrs Nettles about the rucksack, I swear," he whispered. "She worked it out herself."

"I think you did tell," said Fraser. "And after I did you a favour."

"You *never* tell," said Fletcher.

"I didn't."

"So what are you going to do about it?" asked Fraser.

"I could carry your rucksack now," said Henry.

Fraser stood in the rolling mist and thought for a moment, enjoying the worry on Henry's face. "But we're almost back at school."

Henry swallowed.

"I have a better idea. Got any rope on you, Fletch?" said Fraser.

"Of course," said Fletcher, putting on an imitation of Mr Dossit. "Remember, full ... ah ... survival packs ... ah ... boys."

Rope? Why did they want rope? Henry began to panic. He tried to peer round them, hoping to see one of the others. Where were they?

"Then let's tie him to a boulder for the Greybeards to find." Fraser leaned in so close that Henry could smell his breath. "They'll eat him alive."

Henry made a run for it. He pushed through the pair

before they had a chance to react, knocking Fletcher aside and then scrambling along the path.

★

Tadpole reached the forest and flattened herself against a tree trunk with silver bark. She listened to the sounds of the woods, the rustle of fallen leaves as a blackbird fossicked for worms, her own hurried breathing. She was alone. Tadpole took the pendant from her neck and checked the symbols stamped in clay, then threaded her way through the trees, keeping an eye out for the giant boulders shown on the map, Lepus behind her. Deep in the woods, at last she saw some shapes.

"That must be them." Lepus darted towards the mammoth stones.

At the rocks, Tadpole turned to make sure no one had trailed her, then squeezed herself through the gap between the stones. A little further in, Tadpole found the mossy steps where Grandfather had drawn them, and climbed up through the crevice, two at a time, until she burst out into a concealed hollow, covered in grass, and surrounded on all sides by tall ramparts of rock.

And sitting in the middle of the clearing, wrapped in wisps of cloud, with piles of stones for walls and pieces of wood for a roof, was the hut.

"Wow," Lepus gasped.

Tadpole let out a breath. At least now she was hidden for the time being. According to Grandfather, no one ever came to the hollow. No reindeer, no humans and no Greybeards. Certainly not Greybeards. She would get the *specktakulls* as quickly as she could and get out of there. Then she could relax. Tadpole listened out for any sounds of movement. Satisfied, she strode to the front door of Hazel's hut, and pushed it open.

Inside the hut it was dark. In the centre of the cabin was what looked like some sort of stove, with cooking pots on the top. There was also a small eating slab with a bench. Tadpole ignored all that and scanned the hut for the *specktakulls*.

Then a movement caught her eye and she ducked down. On the wall was something shiny. Tadpole stood up and crept closer, jumping back in surprise when she saw another Greybeard hiding inside. Tadpole raised one hand, and then the other. It was just her reflection, like staring into a pool of water, but sharper and clearer than even the stillest lake. She stroked her short beard, bared her teeth and then stuck out her tongue. *How strange I look*, she thought.

Tadpole searched the rest of the hut in a hurry, careful not to knock things over with her bulk. Then she saw the *specktakulls*, just as Snowdrift had described them, on a shelf. She put her pendant down and reached out.

★

Henry staggered down the hill, arms and legs awkward and wild. He could hear Fraser and Fletcher a fair way behind him.

"—e were just joking, Wet—" one of them called.

Henry didn't want to listen, didn't want to stop. He just needed to reach the others. The mist thinned for a moment and he caught sight of dark shapes materializing to his right. Trees. He was near the forest, which meant he wasn't far from the school grounds. Henry stumbled on – and then he tripped.

He toppled off the path and plunged down the slope towards the trees, picking up speed as he tumbled. Round and round, the sound of rushing air filling his ears, expecting at any moment a searing jolt as he smacked into a tree trunk. But it didn't come. Henry scrabbled at the slope with his hands as he plummeted, desperate to grab hold of something – anything – to slow his fall. He felt something (a branch, a root?) and took hold, fingers tight. There was a wrench as it pulled free, but it held. Henry reached up and grabbed it with his other hand. He'd stopped. Then, with horror, Henry realized his legs were kicking free of the ground. He was hanging in the air.

★

A crash sounded over the hollow. Tadpole froze, ears straining. She could hear a groan and the sound of something struggling for breath. Tadpole put the *specktakulls* in her carry sack, making sure to be gentle, and raced out of Hazel's hut, shutting the door behind her and crouching down without a sound. The hair along her back bristled, rising into a crest.

The Greybeard breathed in, straining to smell every drop of mist, grateful for the cover of fog. What was it? She sniffed again. There wasn't a scent – no smell of any animal. And if an animal hadn't crashed through the trees then what had?

"Tadpole, look!" Lepus hissed.

Through a break in the mist, Tadpole saw a shape dangling over the rocky edge, high above the hollow, holding on to a tree root, pulled loose from the earth. A human. The boy scrabbled his legs against the wall of stone, trying to get a foothold. Tadpole could hear him straining – the terror riding on his gasps.

She hesitated for a moment, then bolted for the mossy steps, arms swinging, the soles of her feet brushing the earth. If she strode fast enough, she could reach the boy before he fell.

11

"Help!" Henry cried. His fingers screamed in pain, begging to loosen their grip. He glanced over his shoulder. How far would he drop? He couldn't see. For all he knew, he was hanging off the edge of a cliff. Henry lifted a boot, desperate to find a toehold, his body shaking. Then he tried to walk up the stone, using the root as a rope, but his arms didn't have the strength. He thought he could hear voices coming from higher up. "Help!" he shouted again, his cry swallowed by the mist. He couldn't hold on for much longer.

Then Henry felt a presence. Nearby, in the forest. He couldn't see through the fog, but he wasn't alone – he was sure of it. Someone was out there. Henry tried to lift his head to see. "I'm going to fall!" he called out. "Fletch, Fraser, I'm here!" He felt his grip weakening.

A choking smell drifted through the trees. A musky,

pungent stench – that of a wild animal. Then, making no more sound than a breeze, a colossal shape appeared as if from nowhere, standing right above him on the slope. Henry twisted his head to see a bulky head covered in fur, wide nostrils, dark, squinting eyes. Then the creature lunged at him, thick fingers reaching.

Henry howled as his hands lost their grip.

★

Tadpole held on to the low-hanging branch and swung down. She felt the palm of her hand connect with the boy's arm and snatched at it, her fingers clenching tight. The boy's weight dragged her over the rocky ledge, slamming her chest into the stone. They swung there for a moment, clattering against the rock, the boy dangling in space. The tree branch gave a loud crack. Tadpole clenched her jaw and searched the stone wall with her toes, managing at last to find a foothold.

Her chest ached. She could feel the boy writhing below. Foolish human. If he carried on like that, she'd have to let go. Tadpole heaved on the branch above her head, feeling the wood begin to splinter, then raised a knee, flush with the rock, finally finding a crack with her toes. She pushed down, and then lifted the other leg, edging up the rock, her back straining, shoulders burning. Somehow she wriggled one leg over the ledge and shifted her torso over the top. Still the boy struggled, a strange gargling sound coming from his throat.

The Greybeard heaved with everything she had and started to lift the boy. The boy's panicked jerking began to calm. Now she could feel him shoving on the rock with his feet, trying to help. At last, the weight went slack, and she knew he too had reached the ledge. Tadpole turned to face the boy and his anxious eyes locked on hers. She quickly let go of his arm and leaped behind a tree. *Did I just touch a human?* But she didn't flee – she needed to make sure he was all right.

The boy scrabbled up the hillside on all fours, away from the drop. Then his limbs gave way and he slumped to the ground and just lay there, chest heaving. Tadpole could see he was small, thin – almost hidden underneath the carry sack resting on his back. He wore coverings all over – his feet bound in what looked like leather.

Now the boy rolled himself over on to his back, so he could keep his eyes on her. Terror written all over his face, he looked like he might weep at any moment. He sat there, frozen with dread, his mouth hanging open.

Tadpole swallowed. Did Grandfather's friend Hazel look like this close up too? She glanced about the woods – she really ought to get out of here.

★

Henry kept his eyes on the beast and lay there, panting, his mouth dry. He found he couldn't move his legs or arms; they just wouldn't budge.

The creature was huge, with the build of a gorilla, wide shoulders, and powerful, bulging muscles rippling underneath grey fur. A face of dark skin, eyes wide – alert to danger – large mouth surrounded by a short beard and whiskers. Henry caught a flash of enormous yellow teeth, but he tried to stay calm. Surely, if the creature had wanted to strike out, it would have done so already?

The mist thinned, allowing Henry to study the hollow beneath them. It was a deep crater, carved out of the earth and encircled by a ring of enormous boulders. And there, right in the middle, stood a hut. A bothy with a pitched wooden roof and stone walls. Shrouded in the darkness of the thick forest and dwarfed by the stones that ringed the hollow, it looked old and forgotten. Had this creature been at the bothy when he tumbled down the hillside?

"Thank you," tried Henry, when at last he found his voice. He forced his lips into a weak smile.

The creature's eyes widened a little more. It studied him for a moment. Then it lowered its head in a bow. "Good morning."

"What?" Henry gasped.

"Good morning?" the creature repeated, its voice rasping.

Henry took a deep breath. "You can speak."

"Some. Words."

"Are you a Greybeard?"

The creature shrugged.

Henry slowly took out his phone as it dawned on him that he was in the presence of a creature of legend. He needed to get a photograph but didn't want to startle it, or frighten it away. Henry tapped for the camera and showed the phone to the Greybeard. "Photo?"

Puzzled, it tilted its head, shuffled forwards and then reached out a hand.

All at once, a rustle came from the undergrowth, making them both flinch. A large hare scampered down the hill. Keeping a nervous, watchful eye on Henry, the hare thumped the ground with a long hind leg.

Henry didn't need to speak hare to realize it was a warning. Then he heard them: low voices from further up the hillside, the thud of boots along the forest floor. "Henry!" It was Fraser's voice calling out. "We didn't mean it, honest."

The Greybeard got to its feet in alarm and lunged through the trees, the hare jagging the other way. Henry jabbed at the camera, desperate to catch something, then in an instant they were gone.

Now Fraser and Fletcher appeared over the crest of a mound, torches in hand, searching the misty forest. Their beams found Henry and they stopped.

Fraser gasped. "Henry, don't move!"

"There's a massive drop behind you!" hissed Fletcher.

"Believe me, I know," said Henry. "I stopped just in time."

"Flipping heck. How lucky are you?" said Fraser. "But how on earth did you get down here?"

"I tripped and rolled down the hill," said Henry.

"Numpty," said Fraser.

Glancing over his shoulder, Henry saw thick fog once again blanketed the hollow. "Wait there, I'll come up." He got to his feet and started to climb.

Fletcher looked him up and down. "Are you hurt?"

Henry shook his head. "No, just a few bruises."

"Good." Fraser took off his backpack, handing it to Henry. "Then you can carry this back to school."

Fletcher wrinkled his nose. "Phew, what is that smell?"

Henry opened his mouth, about to explain, but then stopped himself. What if he told them what had just happened? Imagine the commotion a Greybeard sighting would cause. News, camera crews, hordes of curious people, bloggers, video-makers. The Greybeard would be chased off the mountain, or worse. That creature had saved his life. He owed it. "Dead animal?" he suggested.

Fraser covered his nose and mouth with his hand. "Well dead."

"Horrible – let's get out of here," said Fletcher.

Tadpole raced up the hillside through the trees, seeking rocks for camouflage and peak-running as fast as she could. The mist had all but vanished. She spotted Lepus waiting for her, near the crevice. "Phew. We made it," Lepus chirruped. "You said you were up to something risky, but cripes!"

"Tell me about it." Tadpole slumped to the ground, panting. Her legs felt weak. How many slab laws had she just broken? She didn't dare think. She just had to hope those other humans hadn't seen her.

Tadpole leaned over and ruffled the hare's ears. "Thanks for being there, Lepus. Couldn't have done it without you. I'd better get a move on – and not a word to anyone about this. I'd be banished in an instant."

"Hey, no worries. What are companions for?"

Tadpole negotiated her way down the cleft in the stone

towards the entrance slab. She took deep breaths to pull herself together, then knocked on the doorway and waited as it rose.

Deadend glanced at her carry sack, raising a shaggy eyebrow.

Tadpole winced. She'd completely forgotten her story about the droppings!

"I couldn't find any," she spluttered and walked on, trying to avoid the gatekeeper's questioning look.

Back at the den, Tadpole dropped her carry sack off in her room, then went to join Waterworks and Shipshape, a lichen mat still spread out in front of them, a clay pot in the centre. Judging by the number of little discs spread out all over the floor around them, yettiwinks practice was not going well.

Tadpole took a deep breath. Did she look guilty? She hoped her parents wouldn't notice she had the trembles.

"How's it going?" she asked, joining them.

"Not good." Shipshape pressed down with her squidger and sent a wink flying across the table to land on top of Waterworks' head.

"A little lower." He shook the wink to the floor.

"I used to be good – almost as good as Snowdrift," Shipshape sighed.

"I know, Mum." Tadpole gave her a nuzzle.

Shipshape tapped her squidger against her temple.

"It just makes me so annoyed that here we are, wasting our time on this challenge. We should be at work! There are more important things to worry about," she grumbled. "Did you hear that we lost another knot of water?"

"It's almost as if someone's coming in the night and scooping it up, bucket by bucket." Waterworks placed some more winks in front of Shipshape. "Go again."

"What we really need is a different kind of contest." Shipshape squinted at the little discs.

"Rainstorm used one of our laws to challenge you," Tadpole said. "Maybe there's something in the slabs that can help."

"Now why didn't I think of that?" Shipshape slapped her forehead and got to her feet.

When should I tell her about the specktakulls? Tadpole wondered. *And, more to the point, where do I say I got them?*

In the Council chambers, the stools that ringed the enormous stone meeting bench were empty. The family slipped in and closed the door behind them. The carvings rested on a bed of heather in the middle of the room.

Shipshape rubbed her palms on her fur and picked up the first heavy piece of oak, carefully turning it over. "I dare say the bit about contests will be at the back, under Silverback Succession Rules." She squinted at the writing.

"Let me," said Waterworks, taking the slab from her.

Tadpole went over to study the portraits of past silverbacks hanging on the chamber wall, lit by the soft light of insect lanterns. Each leader wore a serious look in their etching, staring forwards, the Stinking Sash hanging across their proud chests, their names carved into the frame, a part of sett history.

At the top of the tree sat Backbone the Wise, his head colossal, his fur silver – the leader of the sett in the times of darkness. Below him frowned his son, Fireball, succeeded by Sideburns, Underfoot and then Backbone the Second. At this point, the line split and went off in a different direction, with the silverbacks Bellbottom, Pothole, Jumpshot and on to a fierce yeti with a sour look to his eyes by the name of Downbeat. Then that line ended, and a new branch began with Moonstruck – a faint smirk etched on her face.

Shipshape came over to Tadpole's side. "Moonstruck is your great-great-great-grandmother. For cycles, the sash has been in our line. All those generations, parent to offspring."

Tadpole traced the portraits down from Moonstruck to where she found her mum – who at least had a smile on her face in her etching. There was still space on the wall below her for more family portraits, starting with Tadpole's. But that didn't seem so likely now.

"How come the silverback line jumps from Downbeat

over to Moonstruck all those cycles ago? How did she become silverback?" asked Tadpole.

"By beating Downbeat in a challenge," said Shipshape. "If I remember my sett history right, a human wounded Downbeat. Caught him out on a ridge. Shot him in the arm with one of their thunderclap sticks. And, with Downbeat permanently injured, Moonstruck saw her chance and took it."

"I've never heard that story before."

"The funny thing is, Downbeat is a distant relation of Rainstorm's."

"No way."

"It's true. Things seem to have come full circle. Life does that sometimes. Our ancestor challenged his, and now he's challenging me."

"It doesn't seem fair."

"The contest law exists to make sure the leadership of the sett stays strong at all times," said Shipshape. "Until the moment comes when the silverback can hand over to the next in line."

"That was supposed to be me," Tadpole sighed.

Now Waterworks spoke up. "From what I read, there's nothing to help us. The laws clearly say that, once the challenge is issued, there's no stopping it. We can't change the type of contest, and it must go ahead at the specified time. Unless the challenger decides to take it back."

"Rainstorm isn't going to do that," said Tadpole.

"Looks like it's more training then," said Waterworks. "We still have a little bit of time."

Now do I tell them about the specktakulls? thought Tadpole, her heart quickening. But, as they left the Council chambers, she lost her nerve and the moment passed.

★

As Henry and the prefects approached the school, Murray appeared out of the mist, heading towards them along the track.

"There you are!" Murray called out. "I turned round and you were gone."

Henry glanced over at Fletcher and Fraser. "I lost the path, slipped and fell."

"No way. Are you all right?"

"Just a scratch or two."

"Lucky." Now Murray saw that Henry was carrying two backpacks. He looked over at Fraser and shook his head.

"What?" Fraser growled.

"Nothing," said Murray. "It's just that Krish and the others have gone to tell Mr Dossit. He's probably on his way here now." He nodded at Henry's shoulders hunched under the extra weight.

Fraser snorted. "Give us it back, Wettie," he said,

reaching for his rucksack.

Having reassured a worried Mr Dossit that he was quite all right – thanks to the prefects, he added, shooting a look at Fletcher and Fraser – Henry found he was actually glad to be in his room. Both he and Murray dumped their rucksacks on the floor and collapsed on to their beds. The ache in Henry's legs from where he'd banged them on the rock was real enough. He hadn't just imagined it all.

"Those prefects didn't mess you about, did they?" said Murray, breaking the quiet.

"They said they were going to tie me to a boulder and leave me there. I think they were joking, but I panicked and tripped and rolled down the hill. But in fairness they did come and find me in the fog."

Murray let out a long breath. "Sorry, Henry. I should have come back to find you myself, and not left it to these two."

Henry sat up and started to untie his bootlaces. "It's OK."

"No, it's not." Murray climbed off his bed and held out his hand. "Friends?"

Henry shook it, with a faint smile. It crossed his mind that if he was going to confide in anyone about what had really happened, Murray was the one.

Then, all at once, a strange moaning sound came from the school grounds. The floorboards quivered and Henry could feel the tremor rise through the frame of his bed. But, before either of the boys could think of moving, the vibrations stopped.

"See!" said Henry. "Same as the other night – I told you."

They went over to the window to look at the barn at the edge of the school grounds. "I think it's coming from that shed."

"Building machinery?" suggested Murray. He gestured at the door. "Anyway, we'd better go, or we'll miss all the biscuits."

Henry lingered by the window a little longer, then chased after his room-mate. He was learning never to pass up the chance of food at Halbrook.

13

Tadpole pushed her way into the exercise yard, the *specktakulls* hidden in her sweaty hand. Greybeards clogged the cave: nearly every yeti in the set had come straight from work to gather round the yettiwinks bench. They burbled to each other in tense clusters. There had been more earth trembles, and worries about the water level in Shadowspring seemed to be on everyone's lips too.

Rainstorm sat on a stool at one side of the clearing, Butterfingers behind him, flanked by Nutcracker and Toothpick. Lukewarm the elder *(she of little enthusiasm)* sat on a bench with the slabs and a sand timer in front of her. Next to her lay the Stinking Sash. Would her mum get to put it back on, Tadpole wondered?

Across the pit stood Shipshape with Waterworks and a cluster of her supporters. Shipshape gave a little wave. Tadpole worked her way round to her.

Waterworks finished rubbing Shipshape's back. "Well, this is it!"

"You can do this, Mum," said Tadpole.

Shipshape gave her a smile. "Any last-minute ideas?"

"Actually, yes." Tadpole swallowed. She opened her fingers to reveal the *specktakulls*. "Wear these."

Shipshape narrowed her eyes. "What on earth are those?"

"A gift from Snowdrift."

"Your grandfather?" asked Waterworks. "What are you talking about?"

"There isn't time to explain," said Tadpole. "But I think these things might help you see."

With her thick fingers, Shipshape picked up the *specktakulls*. She tapped at them. "They're like ice, but warm. Where did you get them?"

"You put them on your nose and look through them," Tadpole explained, ignoring her question.

Waterworks sniffed the *specktakulls*. "But how do you know all this?"

"Because of Snowdrift, because I—" A long blast from Upstage on the horn cut her short. The burbling in the cavern came to a halt. "You just have to trust me," Tadpole whispered. "Those things work."

Shipshape gave her a slow nod, and Tadpole placed the *specktakulls* on her mum's nose, rearranging the fur on her face to hide the frames as best she could.

Shipshape's eyes widened. She looked round the cave, and then down at her hand.

Waterworks leaned in. "*Do* they work?" he murmured.

"Oh yes," Shipshape gasped. "Things are still a little fuzzy, but so much better!"

Now Lukewarm the elder got to her feet, stroking her long beard. "Dear Greybeards, it is said *you can't make a pancake without breaking a few eggs*. We gather here this moon to observe a contest. A challenge for silverback, a contest for the right to wear the Stinking Sash."

There was loud babbling and Lukewarm waited for silence before continuing.

"In one corner, we have our Guardian and challenger, Rainstorm." At this, Hindsight clapped loudly for her cousin – with too much enthusiasm for Tadpole's liking – joined by a smattering of others.

"And on the other we have Shipshape."

Tadpole grinned as the cave broke out into loud cheers. She watched as Rainstorm scowled.

Lukewarm pointed to the yettiwinks mat in the centre of the clearing. "The rules are as follows: each player will take it in turns to shoot their winks into the pot. For each wink potted, the player gets another turn. Miss a wink and the turn is over. The first player to pot all their winks is the winner. If the sand in the timer runs out before either player can do this, it shall be the player with the most winks in the pot. Agreed?"

The crowd gave their assent.

"Are you ready, yettiwinkers?" asked Lukewarm.

Both Rainstorm and Shipshape raised a hand. Lukewarm settled down and got ready to referee. She flipped the timer over, and watched the fine grains of sand as they began to trickle. Then she turned her attention to the yettiwink mat. Upstage gave another trumpet from the horn and the crowd began to cheer.

Peering at the mat through her new *specktakulls*, it was not long before Shipshape began to take charge. She wasted no time shooting one of her winks into the pot with her squidger, and then expertly covered two of Rainstorm's winks with her own, cutting down his options. The Guardian didn't look pleased. "Nice squopping, Mum," Tadpole called out.

Each time either Greybeard fired a wink into the air, there were gasps from the crowd and, when Shipshape potted her second piece to take the lead, the cavern broke out into yodelling. Rainstorm prowled the lichen mat, glowering, as he chose his next shot. He flexed his bony fingers and picked up his squidger. The Guardian selected a wink and pressed down. The disc flew off the lichen mat and hit the rim of the pot. It bounced up, spinning in the air, before dropping back down inside the cup. The crowd gasped. It was an audacious shot. The scores were even.

Then, all at once, Lukewarm stood up and called out, "Wait!" She put the timer on its side, to gasps from the crowd. Shipshape laid down her squidger. Both she and Rainstorm looked over at the referee, puzzled.

Lukewarm pointed at Shipshape's face. "What in sweet reindeer pellets are those things resting on your nose, Shipshape?"

All eyes turned to the silverback. Tadpole felt a flutter in her stomach.

Shipshape took a long breath. "They help me see better," she explained.

"Most peculiar. I can't think why I didn't notice them before," said Lukewarm. There were mutters of agreement from around the cave. "May I?" she asked, holding out a palm.

Shipshape took the *specktakulls* from her nose and handed them over. Lukewarm gave them a sniff, and then ran her fingers over the frames, and the circles of ice. "I've never seen the like in this sett before. Where did you get them?"

Shipshape swallowed. "I…" She paused, then fell silent.

"Well?" insisted Lukewarm.

Tadpole let go of Waterworks' hand and stepped out of the crowd and into the clearing. She felt every head in the cave turn to stare. Her face burned. "I gave them to Mum."

"And where did *you* get them, youngling?" demanded Lukewarm.

Tadpole gulped. "I found them."

"Found them? Where?"

The hollow flashed in Tadpole's mind. She could picture the inside of Hazel's hut. The shelf of books, the stove. "On the peak," she stammered. "Lying on the ground."

"Then they must belong to a human!" Hindsight called out from Rainstorm's side.

There was a collective intake of breath from the onlookers.

"On the mountainside?" gasped Lukewarm. "Then Hindsight is right: these things were not made by a Greybeard hand."

Tadpole hung her head. "Yes, I suppose they could be human."

The room broke into loud bellyaching.

"I object!" said Hindsight. She waited for the grumbling to subside. "Shipshape is benefiting from these human things. She is gaining an advantage from none other than *people*!" Again the cavern filled with complaining.

"Order, please!" Lukewarm shouted. "Order!" She held up a finger while she consulted the slabs, the whole cavern watching.

Shipshape shot a worried look at Tadpole. "*Sorry,*

Mum," Tadpole mouthed back.

"*During a leadership contest, neither competitor may make use of anything which might give them unfair assistance*," Lukewarm read aloud. "The laws are very clear."

There were a few cheers from Rainstorm's supporters. Lukewarm fixed Shipshape with a frown. "I'm sorry, Shipshape, but I must confiscate these human contraptions, and deduct the points you've scored thus far." She held up the *specktakulls* for the crowd to see.

"I understand," Shipshape sighed.

Lukewarm sat down. "Let us restart the competition. Rainstorm, it was your turn. You lead by two winks." She flipped the timer back over.

Rainstorm moved over to reach his wink sitting on the far corner of the mat. Tadpole wondered if he would try to make it in one go. It was a long way off. Rainstorm took his squidger and pressed down. His wink flew into the air and landed just short of the pot. The Guardian had set himself up for an easy one. Tadpole guessed he was banking on Shipshape missing.

Now all eyes turned to Shipshape. She didn't have an easy route, but it was doable. If she potted this one and then managed another, she could even things up. Tadpole gave her dad's hand a squeeze.

Shipshape pressed down but her wink wobbled unsteadily, spun over the pot, and rolled to the far end of the mat. Tadpole groaned – it wasn't even close.

Rainstorm grinned and jabbed confidently with his squidger, but his shot bounced harmlessly off the side of the pot. The Guardian pulled at his beard, angry with himself. A glance at the sand timer told Tadpole that Shipshape was almost out of time. "You can still do this, Mum," she whispered, "but you need to be quick."

Shipshape leaned over the slab, narrowing her eyes, her whiskers almost touching the mat. There wasn't a sound from the gathered crowd.

This is it, thought Tadpole.

Shipshape held her breath, pressed down... Her wink soared ... and flew...

"Ouch!" cried Hindsight, rubbing her eye as the wink bounced off her face and fell to the ground.

The crowd gasped.

"Time!" announced Lukewarm as the last grains dropped through the timer. She picked up the pot. "I declare Rainstorm the winner – by two winks!" Stunned silence greeted the announcement, and then the cavern broke out into respectful clapping. Rainstorm acknowledged the applause with both hands raised. Shipshape dropped her head.

Tadpole ran over and held her tight.

"I just couldn't see, Tadpole. I just couldn't..."

When Lukewarm took the sash from the table and held it out to the Guardian, Tadpole felt ill. Rainstorm lifted the sash, unable to keep the smile from his face, and lowered it over his chest. Hindsight and some of the others gathered round to congratulate him. Then the new silverback held his hand in the air and the cavern fell silent.

"I am sorry that your eyes have failed you, Shipshape, and that it came to a challenge. Though we may not always agree on everything, I admire what you have done for this sett." He gave Shipshape a bow.

"Hear, hear!" shouted a voice.

Shipshape acknowledged Rainstorm's words with a sad nod.

Now Rainstorm turned to address the rest of the crowd. "My sweet-smelling friends, it is said that *cold showers bring forth flowers*. Now is the time for change! I say we cannot

113

and will not allow humans to interfere with our way of life."

"No humans!" someone cried, and the cavern broke into loud cheers. "No humans!"

"It is bad enough that their filth dirties Shadowspring. We Greybeards must work harder and harder to keep the water clean." Rainstorm paused to let his words sink in. "Then each cycle they come to the mountains in growing numbers. Again we had a large trampling of human younglings over the ranges. And more people means more risk of our sett being discovered."

Tadpole swallowed. She thought about the human boy in the hollow. About grabbing his arm. Speaking to him.

Rainstorm continued. "Our hare companions reported at least four separate groups of humans marching the ranges – and one lot almost discovered Scapegoat while he was out foraging. By lucky chance, he got away but it was a close call, and he had to leave all his toadstools behind."

Anxious murmurs filled the hall. Scapegoat *(he who always gets the blame)* acknowledged Rainstorm's words with an embarrassed wave.

"With the Collective soon to arrive, I must therefore command that, in the interests of security, all visits to the surface have now to be approved by myself or Deadend, effective immediately." A nervous muttering spread across the Greybeards.

"A wise precaution," said Hindsight above the noise.

"We will keep you informed. Hear me as I speak."
Rainstorm sat back down.

"He doesn't waste any time making his mark does he,
Grandfather?" grumbled Tadpole. She felt for the pendant,
searching the hair around her neck. There was nothing. She
patted her chest and looked down. There was no cord, no
smooth clay. No map. It was gone.

Tadpole's heart skipped a beat. *Could it have fallen off on
the way back? Had the cord snapped?* She saw herself peak-
running through the forest, up the mountain, bounding as
fast as she could.

Tadpole retraced her steps in her head. *When did she
last use the necklace?* She thought back to the hollow,
going inside the hut. Reaching for the *specktakulls*…

As she gazed round the burbling Greybeards, Tadpole
felt cold. She knew exactly where she'd left the pendant.
The pendant with the map to the sett on it.

★

Far below the earth, along one of the waterways that criss-
crossed the globe, came the canoe of the Sasquatch Rapid
Reaction Volunteers, Inke *(he with stained fingers)* at the
helm.

"Ranke, progress report, if you please," he commanded.

"Sir!" Ranke *(she who is rotten)* turned to face her leader
at the back of the canoe. "Speed ten pebbles and steady.

Distance to Greybeards approximately fourteen moons. Next landing spot fifty strides, sixty at the most."

"Spratt! Set the stroke to twelve pebbles, if you please. Let's reach that landing spot quicker if we can."

"Sir!" said Spratt *(he who eats no fat)*.

"Grubb, rations status!"

"As planned, sir, though we've finished the last of the cricket juice," said Grubb *(she covered in dirt)*.

Inke frowned. "What, already? Then it's plain water from here on in. But not to worry: we've trained for these conditions."

"Sir!"

★

In their own canoe, the yeti of the Hibagon sett leaned back on cushions of soft silkworm thread and when they felt up to it, stroked the stream with their paddles. They'd been down in the waterway for many moons, long ahead of the others, and were happy to take the water as it flowed. It was their way.

"I sniff out, with my little snout something beginning with T," said Humm *(she who makes tuneful sounds behind closed lips)*.

"T, eh?" said Curde *(he who loves cheese)* with a yawn.

"Give up?" asked Humm after some time, when she thought she heard Curde snoring.

Curde opened one eye. "What letter was it again?"

"T."

"Tunnel," said Curde at last.

"Well done." Humm yawned, stretching out her arms. "Your turn."

Curde rubbed his eyes. For a while, there was no sound but the gurgling of the stream. "I sniff out, with my little snout something beginning with W."

"W?" Humm leaned back into the cushions. "Now let me think..."

★

While the other Barmanou paddled, Winkk *(she who opens and closes one eye)* struck flint against stone until she was able to light the wick of the beeswax lamp. By the flickering glow, she read over the message from Snott the silverback *(he with runny nose)* to the Collective. It was a cry of warning. The once-mighty glaciers shrank cycle on cycle. Soon hardly anything would remain. What then?

But, also carved into the tree bark, Snott proposed a solution. A radical idea that would turn the yeti world on its head:

The time has come to confront the humans. Meet them head-on. Bring them to heel before they ruin the Earth.

Winkk wondered just how the others would receive it.

15

It had been seven moons since the Stinking Sash had been stripped off her mum's shoulders with barely a ruffling of fur, or so it seemed to Tadpole. The smell of fresh gnat biscuits wafted from the kitchen; whitewash grew brushstroke by brushstroke over tunnel walls; and builder Greybeards hurried to repair the damage caused by the trembles and finish the Collective lodgings, newly carved out of rock. Shipshape was now in charge of accommodation. Waterworks was back in Shadowspring – the water level down another two knots. Word was beginning to spread that humans were somehow to blame. But, other than that, everyone carried on as usual. Had Shipshape's reign meant so little to the others?

After she'd got over the shock of the yettiwink match, it dawned on Tadpole that she was no longer next in line for silverback. She also realized she didn't feel any better for it.

If she was honest, there was a sour taste in her mouth – was it the flavour of disappointment? Had she wanted to be a leader all along? Tadpole pushed the thought from her head. It was too late now. Butterfingers was next in line, as Rainstorm's son. "Earth Mother help us all," groaned Tadpole. Nice enough youngling, but without an original thought in his head.

Tadpole got orders from Hindsight – whom Rainstorm had promoted to Guardian – that she was to join the painting team. Paintbrush and paintpot in hand, ladder over her shoulder, Tadpole trudged along the tunnel on her way to the sett entrance. She passed the library, empty but for a few elderly Greybeards, and the kitchen patch where Grasshopper the gardener *(she who likes greens)* was watering her tomatoes and lettuces under the glare of a multitude of lamps.

In the main tunnel, Tadpole set up her ladder and climbed to the top step. She dipped her brush and began dabbing. White globs of paint fell from the ceiling like drops of rain. As she painted, she couldn't shake what Rainstorm had said at the yettiwinks match from her head: *We cannot and will not allow humans to interfere with our way of life.* It had kept Tadpole up in her nest night after night.

There was no hiding from it. She needed to get that pendant back, and sooner rather than later. If the boy found out about Hazel's place, then other humans were bound to know about the hut too. It wouldn't take them long to notice the pendant. And how long would it then take them to work out that it was a map and be curious about following the trail – a path that would lead them right to the sett door? Rainstorm and Lukewarm might have been willing not to punish her over the *specktakulls*, but revealing the location of the sett? Tadpole dreaded to think. She had to get back out on to the mountainside.

★

A whole week had passed since the tramp and Henry just couldn't get the image of the Greybeard out of his mind. As he pulled on his running gear that morning, he thought about the Greybeard's dark eyes, a little too close together, questioning and intelligent. Her flat nose, wide nostrils flaring as she drew breath. The size of her. Huge thick arms. The Greybeard ran upright too from what he'd seen, not like an ape. So just what were they?

After the tramp, Henry had managed to dig out a book in the school library: *The Greybeard: Legend and Fact*. There were many stories: climbers gripped by a horrible feeling of eeriness – of unexplained terror. Mountain trampers who saw shapes in the mist that came with the crunch of footfall. In one historical encounter, a man let off a shot from his musket, claiming to have wounded the beast.

Though the book was full of half-sightings, there didn't seem to be much solid evidence. A couple of footprints in the snow were all anyone had ever found. The theories people had to explain Greybeards were wild too: a ghost, a stranded yeti, a type of bear.

While Murray was still out of the room, Henry took another quick look at his photo. He swiped through his gallery, through the shots from the top of Ben Bell, until he found the Greybeard. It was blurred but there was no denying it was there. A large grey back, massive arms, legs in full flight. None of this was supposed to be real, but it was. And he didn't dare share it with anybody. So what next? Henry felt a twist in his stomach. Even though the thought of being so close to the creature again made him uneasy, he knew he had to see if he could find the Greybeard again. He wouldn't rest until he did.

It was just like the Pirate Galleon. Henry remembered the time his dad took him to the local fairground when he was little. After thirty years, the park was retiring the pirate ship and Dad wanted to ride on it one last time, even donning a pirate hat for the occasion.

Henry hadn't liked the way the bar closed over his lap, locking him on to the ship. But he was glad for it as the ship started swinging, climbing higher and higher with each swing, only to plunge back down. Henry felt lurch after lurch of dread, and closed his eyes, wishing for the ride to end. But when at last the ship slowed down to a stop, and they got off, Henry found himself tugging at his father's hand, eager to join the queue again.

His thoughts were interrupted when Murray opened the door and threw his towel and toothbrush on the bed. "Come on – those prefects will have us on extra laps if you don't hurry up."

They clattered down the dorm stairs and joined the others out on the front lawn, already stretching their legs and doing warm-ups.

"Hey, Murray, isn't that your dad?" said Krish as a muddy four-wheel drive crunched down the driveway and pulled to a stop beside them.

"What's he doing here?" mumbled Murray.

A thin, wiry man hopped down from the car and gave a wave as Murray went over.

"Don't you think Murray's dad looks like an ostrich?" whispered Bony.

Henry stifled a smile. Bony wasn't wrong. Mr Roth did look like a bird: bulging eyes peering out from behind round glasses, head nodding and bobbing at the end of a long neck, a pale, thin mouth turned down at the sides almost like a beak.

"You should see Murray's house. Huge. Bigger than Halbrook Hall," said Krish.

"Hold on, his family lives near here?" Henry asked.

"Oh yeah, just down the road," said Bony. "On the other side of the woods."

"And he makes Murray board?"

Krish laughed. "Yeah, Murray says it's all about turning him into a man."

"Henry, Dad wants to meet you," Murray called out.

Henry jogged over and held out his hand. "Henry Wetwood."

Murray's dad gave it a firm shake. "So you're the new room-mate?"

"Yes, Mr Roth."

Roth craned his neck to study Henry. "A bit late in the term to start at Halbrook, isn't it?"

"My parents had to take a job abroad. They're publishers."

"How fascinating." Roth sounded anything but interested.

Over Roth's shoulder, Henry saw Mr Dossit come out of his cottage and cross the drive to join them. "I thought it … ah … was your car, Mr Roth."

"Ready for our meeting, headmaster? Jarvis and MacNeil should be here any moment."

"Ah yes … I have, ah … some things I need to talk about."

"Save it for down at the plant," said Roth. "Henry was just telling me about his parents' publishing company.

We should have him to stay this weekend, Murray. I'm sure he'd like to see the manor."

"That would be nice, Mr Roth," said Henry.

"Excellent. I'm sure Mr Dossit will give you permission," said Roth.

"Happy to," said the headmaster.

Roth climbed back into his car. "I'll see you down there, Dossit." He started up the car and drove off.

Mr Dossit turned to Henry. "So your parents ... are publishers?"

"Yes, sir."

"Working on a book myself as it ... ah ... happens. Nowhere near finished unfortunately."

"What's it about, headmaster?" asked Henry.

Mr Dossit's eyes sparkled. "A history of our wonderful school. I've just reached Hazel Halbrook – the last in the Halbrook line. She was my headmistress when I ... was a student here in the 1980s – fascinating person." Mr Dossit let out a sigh. "Though what happened to her ... ah ... after she retired is a mystery."

Henry was surprised. "You went to Halbrook School?"

"Oh yes." Mr Dossit beamed. But his smile faded away as another four-wheel drive crunched down the driveway and slowed beside them. The passenger window lowered and a voice from the darkened interior called out, "Ready, Dossit?"

"Right … ah … you are," said the headmaster as the car carried on towards the barn. He gave Henry an encouraging smile. "I'll let you in on a little secret, Wetwood. Absolutely hated Halbrook at first. Never felt so alone in my … ah … life. Missed my home … missed my family. But I settled in soon enough. You'll come to like it here too, Wetwood, you'll see."

"Thank you, sir."

"I'd best go. Enjoy your run."

Henry watched as the car stopped at the barn, and two men in suits carrying briefcases got out. The door to the shed slid open, and then closed before Mr Dossit had a chance to get there. Henry saw him knocking on the door to be let in.

Now Fraser and Fletcher came down the steps. "Off you go, juniors, three laps!" Fletcher waved a clipboard. "I'm counting."

"And no stopping or you'll be running extra," added Fraser, giving a blast on his whistle.

Henry and Murray broke into a jog. "Sorry my dad put you on the spot earlier, Henry. He can be quite embarrassing," Murray panted.

"All parents are embarrassing," said Henry. "You haven't seen my father watch Arsenal on TV."

It was soon clear that the other boys were more used to cross-country running than Henry, and halfway through the first lap Bony, Krish and the rest were way out in front. Even Murray had left him behind.

As Henry followed the waist-high fence round the school boundary, he peered into the forest on the other side of the railings. He kept his eyes on the shadows between the trees – a part of him wished that he'd catch sight of a mysterious shape again.

Round the back of the barn, Henry slowed to a walk to catch his breath, avoiding a giant pipe that came out of the wall of the shed and disappeared into the ground. Then he heard raised voices and saw the back door of the shed was open.

"Don't be ridiculous, Dossit."

"How else do you think your English department is going to be built?"

"But … ah … what about the … tremors?"

"Teething problems."

"I still think … we should stop until we know more. I'm concerned."

"Too late for that now."

"We've invested far too much. Our plans will go ahead!"

"Make your man see sense, Roth."

As he passed the door, Henry saw the headmaster surrounded by Roth and the men in suits – whom he assumed were Jarvis and MacNeil. When they caught sight of him jogging past, the group fell silent at once.

Roth marched over and shut the door.

Henry picked up his pace, rounding the corner of the barn back towards the playing fields. Whatever was going on in there, thought Henry, they were arguing – and it was clear they hadn't wanted him to hear what they were saying. *Our plans will go ahead.* Something told him those plans weren't to do with the new English block.

16

That afternoon, a gang of Greybeards marched past Tadpole's ladder towards the sett entrance, Toothpick leading the way and Nutcracker bringing up the rear. There was an urgency to their striding, it occurred to Tadpole. They were off to do something important. More important than whitewashing anyway.

"Go on, say it – I need to mind my own business, right?" Tadpole whispered to Snowdrift.

There was no answer, of course. The pendant was gone.

But, if a group of Greybeards were leaving the sett, maybe this was her chance to get out? Tadpole climbed down the ladder, leaving her paintpot and brush, and crept after the trooping Greybeards, keeping to the shadows.

At the sett entrance, Tadpole dropped down and hid as Toothpick marshalled the Greybeards into two ranks. Deadend waited.

"Attention!" Nutcracker barked.

The group stood straight. Now Deadend walked down the line, inspecting them one by one, a look of disdain on his face. "Is this really the best we can do?"

"It's all Rainstorm said could be spared," said Toothpick.

As Deadend reached Backfire *(she with noisome bottom vapours)*, she let out a nervous gust, and the cavern filled with the foulest smell. Tadpole and the others took deep, approving breaths.

"Better not do that while we're out peak-running," said Scallywag.

"Talk about *blowing* your cover," said Eggnog *(she fond of eggs and cream)*.

"Backfire, you really are throwing caution to the *wind*," added Dishcloth *(he who likes cleaning)*.

Backfire and the others broke into soft gurgles.

"Smarten up!" growled the gatekeeper.

The troop of Greybeards looked at their feet and fell silent.

"Silly yeti," Deadend continued. "We have an important job to do. You must keep your wits about you – understand?"

"Yes, Deadend," came the reply.

"And you keep quiet about this in the sett too."

"Yes, gatekeeper."

Deadend checked the slate in his hands. "Toothpick

and Nutcracker, I want you to head over to the rock falls – you'll almost certainly run into some humans there, so I want some Greybeards who know what they're doing. Make sure you're well and truly hidden."

"Yes, Deadend," the guard yeti answered as one.

"As for the rest of you…"

Tadpole listened as the gatekeeper gave out his orders to the others. Rainstorm had stopped visits to the surface except for the most essential things. So why were these Greybeards going out?

"Return to the crevice to report before dusk," finished Deadend.

"Before dusk," the Greybeards replied.

With a satisfied grunt, Deadend began pulling at the rope to raise the doorway slab. Nutcracker and Toothpick were the first to leave, slipping into the gloom without a sound, and, seeing them head into the crevice, the rest of the Greybeards surged towards the opening in a mass.

"Stop pushing," complained Dishcloth.

Tadpole saw her chance. Without thinking it through, she climbed out from behind the rock and blended in with the throng as they elbowed their way into the darkened fissure.

★

We've driven into the village today and found a place where we can get internet. Karman refuses to have Wi-Fi in his home (which really is in the middle of nowhere) or anything modern like that. No TV, heats all his water on the stove. There's absolutely no mobile phone signal either. Takes a little getting used to. Dad had to argue with him to let us use our laptops at all – he wanted us to write everything out by hand. He finally agreed but has been a little grumpy about it to say the least. Work on the book has been slow.

Hope that you and your room-mate are getting along, and that you're settling into Halbrook.

It must be wonderful being surrounded by all that countryside. Remember our trek round the Roman Way?

Love you, miss you.

Mum

PS Dad says that boarding school is all about standing on your own two feet and to make the most of it!

As he left the school building after last period, Henry's fingers hovered over the keyboard on his phone. He was desperate to tell them about what he'd seen in the forest. But how to start? They'd think he'd lost his mind.

Down on the football pitch, Mrs Nettles had the players running in and out of cones, warming up for the afternoon's match. Clumps of boys were already settling down in the late sun on the grass beyond the touchlines.

Henry spotted Murray and Bony wandering down to join the spectators, but instead he went over and leaned on the fence, bringing up the photo again. The shape on the screen still gave him the chills. Henry thought back to the look in the Greybeard's eyes. There was something familiar there. Was it a feeling of being all alone?

Could he really find the creature again?

Henry turned his gaze to the trees beyond, light slanting through the branches, birds calling. Mum was right: there was something wonderful about being in the country. He smiled, remembering that family walk along the Roman Way. He'd never realized that Mum and Dad were a couple of nature presenters in disguise.

★

The family had stopped on the narrow white trail cutting through farmland to take photos of the sea of yellow around them. "For thousands of years, people have been walking this chalk path," gasped Henry's mum. "I just love these fields of mustard seed."

"And look, Henry!" Dad crouched down. He showed Henry a snail with a black swirl on the side of its shell. "Did you know the Romans brought this species of snail to England for eating, and they've been here ever since."

"Smell that air," added his mum, breathing in

appreciatively. "We should really get out into the country more often."

But, since then, they rarely had done.

★

And now Henry felt the woods calling to him. Somewhere through those trees lay the secret hollow, ringed with stones, the bothy hidden inside. The Greybeard had been at the bothy the other day. Was there a slim chance it might go there again?

Scanning the woodland, Henry spotted the stream running alongside the fence and into the trees. He noticed it was roughly in line with the mountain trail they'd taken to Ben Bell the other day – he could see where the track started further along the grounds. If he kept to the stream, didn't that mean there was a good chance he'd hit the stone boulders? Did he dare?

PS Dad says … to make the most of it!

Henry slipped the phone back in his pocket and glanced round the school grounds. Another lorry growled down the drive towards the shed, Mrs Nettles had blown the whistle to start the match, and hammering and drilling came from the building site. Surely no one would notice if he climbed over the fence and drifted into the trees? He had just over an hour before the dinner bell. If he found the hollow and got back before then, there was little chance anyone would miss him. The moment he felt like he was out of his depth, even just a little bit, he'd turn round. Henry made up his mind, his breath quickening at the idea.

He tightened the straps on his school bag, so it sat snug against his back, took another glance around, then stepped up on the first railing. He swung his other leg over and straddled the top railing like a horse, before dropping down on the other side, stumbling as he landed. He scampered into the woods and hid behind a tree trunk. Peering back at the school, he half expected a shout of, "Stop, you there!" but no one had noticed.

Making sure he took in some landmarks as he hiked – a fallen tree, a peculiar-shaped rock – Henry pushed on through the trees, the leaves already beginning to turn with the first hints of autumn. He chose to ignore the nagging doubts in his mind and focused on the whistle and call of the birds. He met the bank of the stream, the water gurgling gently. The stream sat quite low, judging by the height of the banks, but the water was so clear that Henry could see the rocks on the bottom, and ribbons of weed waving gently in the current. No plastic bottle lids in sight. He carried on, shadowing the brook deeper and deeper into the woods.

17

At last, in the middle of the forest, Henry saw the jumble of enormous stones. He felt his heart begin to beat faster. This had to be it. At first glance, the boulders seemed an impenetrable wall, but he explored a little more and found a dark crevice, big enough to squeeze through. It looked like a cave. He studied the gloom for a moment longer, starting to lose his nerve.

"Sir Wetwood rolls a six. Boldly inspects the hollow, seeking answers," he muttered aloud, and pushed in before he had a chance to change his mind.

The crevice went in a fair way, curving round. Then Henry saw them. Steps: carved out of stone, and covered in moss like a secret staircase. Henry tiptoed up them, squeezing between the boulders, and emerged in the hollow.

He glanced about the clearing, ready to turn round and run back out if he needed to. But there was nothing there.

No Greybeard. Of course, it had been a silly idea.

In fairness, the hollow looked completely different from how it had the week before – more welcoming. Dappled light flickered over a tiny meadow covered with long grass and wildflowers. There was a small pond almost hidden by overhanging branches, and the boulders that surrounded the clearing were the rich green of the moss and lichen that covered them. The rock walls towered on all sides, seeming much higher when viewed from ground level. Henry spotted the rock face where he'd hung. He was lucky he hadn't fallen – that drop was a leg-breaker or worse. He certainly owed the Greybeard a great deal.

Henry turned his attention to the bothy. Above the door, burned into a piece of wood, was the name BUDGE. Was there someone still living here?

Henry glanced at his watch. He still had time before he had to be back. "Hello?" he called out. He knocked on the door and waited. When there was no reply, he turned the handle and pushed it open. Henry froze. He'd been expecting a bare, cold hut, perhaps a wooden bench, maybe a table. But nothing like this. 'Budge' was utterly wonderful. The bothy was small and cosy – not an inch of space wasted, nothing out of place. Just big enough for one, like the cabin of a sailing boat. Though soft dust covered every surface, Henry could see the cabin had once been cared for and loved. It was a warm home, not a walker's refuge. And the books! Budge was absolutely crammed with them. Shelves of books covered one end of the hut from the wooden floor to the peaked ceiling – a wonderful muddle of colours and titles. It was like a second-hand bookshop: musty, but warm and welcoming.

Henry glanced over his shoulder to make sure he was truly alone, then crept in. He ran his fingers over leather-bound histories and volumes of plays. There were dozens of paperbacks with muted orange covers; heavy dictionaries; green, cloth-bound studies of birds with embossed gold lettering; and rows of dog-eared children's books, worn from the touch of many hands.

In the middle of the bothy there was a pot-bellied stove and flue, and above the door a small loft. Henry tested the wooden ladder, went up a couple of rungs and investigated the space above to find a bed, sheets still neatly tucked in.

Then, on the small table below, Henry discovered a stack of tidy notebooks, the red leather covers faded and soft. The dusty books looked as if they hadn't been touched in years, but next to them on the table sat a fountain pen, as if the hand that held it had just finished writing and laid it down. Henry picked a notebook off the top of the pile and opened it. The title page read *The Startling Adventures of Sebastian Finch. A Children's Novel by Hazel Halbrook.* Hazel Halbrook – wasn't she the very person Mr Dossit had said he was researching? This was just too peculiar.

Henry flipped to the first page.

Chapter One

Sebastian Finch shifted his bag strap to stop it cutting into his shoulder and hastened his steps down the country road. He was beginning to regret getting out of the coach to walk – the idea had seemed a good one in the light of day. But now he watched the dark shadows of the woods and could hear the creaking and scratching of the branches growing louder. He should have paid more attention to the bemused shake of the coach driver's head. If it had been light, Sebastian would have seen the carpets of bluebells that covered the woods. But, in the darkness, who knew what lurked in the thick trees on either side of the road?

A young sailor, a prison, an escape across stormy seas. Henry was three pages in before he realised. And he knew that meant it was good. He checked the last notebook in the pile and found a tidy *THE END*. Her book was finished then.

Henry pictured Hazel Halbrook the headmistress in her retirement years: long grey hair, glasses, chewing the end of her fountain pen, a fire in the stove, the kettle whistling with the promise of tea. Writing the final words of the story with a flourish of her pen and placing it on top of the pile.

But where was she now?

It really was time he thought about going back. He hadn't met the Greybeard as he'd hoped, that was true, but what a find Budge was! Who'd have thought such a place even existed? Henry's fingers toyed with the notebooks on the desk. Imagine – he could be the first person ever to read it. Did he dare borrow a notebook and take it back to Halbrook? Henry decided against it. He also decided against telling Mr Dossit about Hazel's bothy – not yet anyway. For the moment, he liked the idea of it staying his secret – just like the Greybeard.

Henry took a last look round the bothy, drinking it all in before going. It was then that he spotted a handprint stamped into the dust on one of the shelves. He hovered his own hand over it – the handprint in the dust was massive. Henry felt a chill. So the Greybeard *had* been there!

Now Henry noticed there was a pendant sitting on the shelf, made from white clay, glazed and smooth, attached to a woven cord. He picked it up, then pulled his head back. It smelled like cat wee. Was this the Greybeard's necklace? Henry turned it round in his hand. One side was plain but on the other there were some interesting shapes pressed into the clay. He took a quick photo and dropped the phone back in his pocket.

All at once, another stronger smell invaded the room. Henry turned to find a huge figure blocking the doorway.

Tadpole stood and watched the boy, the fur on the back of her neck stiffening. He reminded her of a reindeer standing frozen. He was fearful, cornered. And in his hands was her pendant. Had he understood what the markings were?

Tadpole took a breath and ducked through the doorway, trying to remember the right word to say. "Goodbye," she whispered.

The boy looked stunned. "Hello?"

"Hello," Tadpole corrected herself.

She pointed to the pendant in his hands. "Me. That."

The boy looked down at the necklace. Then he shuffled forwards and held it out with trembling hands.

Tadpole grabbed the pendant and draped it round her neck. She thought hard. "Thank you."

"*Sweet reindeer pellets,*" gasped Snowdrift, materializing.

"*A human boy!*"

"It's OK, Grandfather, I've met him before," said Tadpole. "I think he's all right."

"*I should never have put you in harm's way.*"

Now the boy said something Tadpole didn't understand. She tilted her head, puzzled.

"*Of all the silly grandfathers…*" said Snowdrift. "*I blame myself.*"

"Shush, Grandfather," said Tadpole. "I'm trying to understand what he's saying."

The boy tried again. "How do you know how to speak?"

"*He's asking how you know his language,*" Snowdrift translated.

Tadpole paused, struggling to find the words. "Grandfather know woman words." Tadpole touched the pendant and gestured at the hut. "Woman friend."

"Where is your grandfather's friend now?"

Tadpole considered his question. She went outside, beckoning him to follow.

★

Still keeping his distance, Henry followed the Greybeard out of the bothy, over to the far end of the clearing. The creature gestured at a mound of earth covered in grass and wildflowers. "Woman. Hazel."

Henry stared at the grave, somewhat downhearted at

the idea of Hazel's passing. But then he remembered: here he was standing next to a real, live Greybeard! Henry tapped at his chest. "My name is Henry. HEN-RY."

The Greybeard seemed to understand, tapping its chest and burbling something that Henry didn't quite catch. He gave a shrug. The Greybeard thought for a moment, then went over to the pond, waving at Henry to follow. The creature searched the water, then pointed a thick finger at the weeds. Swimming among the green fronds were little black commas. The Greybeard pointed at them and then tapped its chest again.

"Woman. Tadpole."

"Tadpole?" Henry tried.

"Yerrssss." The creature grinned. She went back and sat down on a rock near the grave and plucked a flower from the mound. Tadpole was about to eat it, but instead offered it to Henry.

"Thank you, but no."

At this, Tadpole just shrugged her enormous hairy shoulders and popped it in her mouth. The sound of her munching, and the way she snorted while she ate, reminded Henry of a hungry horse, gentle and calm. The reek coming from her fur was quite something, like a field full of wet dung.

Henry had so many questions. He decided to start with a simple one. "How many are there of you? How many?"

At first, the Greybeard didn't seem to understand. She tilted her head, and then she held up two hands and flashed them seven times.

"Seventy," gasped Henry. He tried to imagine what seventy large, hairy creatures looked like all together. What they *smelled* like. "Where do you live? Where is your home?"

Tadpole wobbled her head and pointed at Henry. "Where you home?"

"I live in Halbrook Hall." He gestured through the woods in what he thought was the direction of the school. "Well, actually, I don't live there. I'm just stuck there for a while. My real home is in London. London? It's a big city a long way from here. City?" Henry tried. He smiled at the look of confusion on Tadpole's face.

"Talk too many," said the Greybeard.

"True," admitted Henry, annoyed with himself. Of course she wouldn't know all those words. Maybe he could draw pictures to explain. *Better yet, I can show her*, he thought. He got out his phone and found the gallery. Then he inched closer, trying to breathe through his mouth.

"Those are my friends, Li and David. Friends." Henry showed her a photo.

The Greybeard's eyes widened. "Human there?"

"Just a picture. Picture." Henry swiped over to the next photo. "There's us at school."

Tadpole watched Henry as he scrolled through several photos, and then reached for the phone herself and began swiping her forefinger over the screen rapidly, Henry giving a running commentary.

"That's my room … a classic sports car I saw on the street … this massive cucumber Mum and I got at the supermarket … a cute cat meme … a video of the winning slap in the world slapping competition … a funny-shaped cloud that looks like a nuclear bomb has just gone off…" Henry paused when his parents came up and Tadpole stopped scrolling. It was a photo he had taken on the train up here. "And that's my mum and dad. Mother. Father."

Tadpole seemed to notice the croak in his voice. She pointed at the photo. "Good. Mother. Father."

"Yes, good," Henry agreed. "What about your mother and father?"

Tadpole considered his words. "Mother see not good. Eyes bad."

"I'm sorry to hear that," said Henry.

Suddenly Tadpole rose to her feet. She looked up at the sky and then at the shadows made by the tree trunks. "Tadpole go now."

"Do you have to?"

"Tadpole trouble."

"Will you come here again? Here?" Henry pointed at Tadpole and then at the bothy.

Tadpole seemed to understand. "No. Big no."

"Me too," admitted Henry. "Well, it was nice meeting you. I'll never forget." He held out his hand.

Tadpole looked down at his hand, puzzled. Instead, she tapped her hand on her chest and then on her head. "Goodbye. Hen-ree."

Henry returned the gesture, tapping his chest and his head, making the Greybeard smile. "Goodbye, Tadpole."

The Greybeard stopped at the top of the stairs and gave Henry a last look, and then she was gone.

Henry went back to the little refuge and pulled the door shut. He would definitely keep the place a secret. It somehow seemed Hazel would have wanted it that way. Right now, Henry needed to sneak back into Halbrook without anyone noticing, He hoped he hadn't missed the dinner bell – he was starving.

★

Tadpole ran through the forest, arms swinging, striding from tree trunk to tree trunk in a blur. At the edge of the trees, she dropped down, held her breath and listened. Not a sound. She took a deep sniff. The way up the mountainside was clear so she sprang up the hill and into the scrub, keeping low as she ran.

Tadpole was halfway back to the sett when she caught a scent of nearby Greybeard riding on the wind – one of Deadend's team, it had to be. Tadpole dropped down in a flash, wedging herself in the space between two rocks. Peering out from her hiding place, she scanned the jumble of grey stone that lay tumbled down the slope, as if scattered by a giant, unseen hand. Now she could see two shapes hiding on the other side of the steep gully below her. It was Toothpick and Nutcracker. Tadpole remembered they'd been sent to the rock falls.

Tadpole's heart raced. Could they see her? She didn't think so. It looked like they were lying in wait. But for what?

Before long, at the top of the gully, two more figures appeared, picking their way along the path through the strewn rocks. Humans. The one in front bright yellow, the other red – dressed up like a couple of oversized flowers, making their way back down from the mountain. The people used sticks to help themselves along and, even from where she was sitting, Tadpole could hear heavy feet clomping on rock.

Now Tadpole caught a sound and tilted her head. Then on the breeze she heard it again – but only just. A sorrowful hum wafting over the gorge, deep and low. She toyed with her necklace.

"*Is that a Murmur?*" said Snowdrift. "*Is someone Murmuring?*"

Tadpole gasped. Murmuring. Toothpick and Nutcracker.

The humans pushed on, picking their way through the boulders. Tadpole could see they were now almost in line with the two Greybeards hiding in the shadows. Then, as the Murmur reached them, the first human suddenly stopped and held out an arm. The companion drew to a halt too, their limbs tense in an instant. They moved closer to each other, seeking the other out without taking their gaze off the gorge.

The humans stood back to back, searching the fallen rock, certain now that they were not alone – that something was coming. The Murmuring rose, louder and louder, until the whole gorge filled with vibrations.

Tadpole could hear the humans babbling to each other, their tongue rapid and shrill. Then, all at once, they bolted, scrambling down the hill, stumbling and awkward, arms flailing. One tripped and fell, tumbling to the ground. Even gripped with panic, the other human turned round and ran back to help. Then they hobbled on, arm in arm, supporting each other. Tadpole could almost taste their terror.

Tadpole thought of Hen-ree. What would he look like running for his life, a terrible Murmur shaking his chest?

When the people staggered out of sight over the next ridge, Toothpick slipped out from her hiding spot and peak-ran back towards the sett entrance. She wondered if the sett guard felt bad at all. Did she care? There was no sign of Nutcracker. Perhaps he'd already drifted away unnoticed.

Tadpole sat back with a thump. So all the Greybeards at the entrance earlier were out to scare humans off the mountainside. When she got back to the sett, she'd have to tell her mum.

"*This is Rainstorm's doing*," Grandfather muttered. "*And I don't like it one bit.*"

Tadpole needed to get back to the main entrance and wait for the others to gather so she could sneak in with them undetected. She got to her feet and took to the slope, arms swinging, feet meeting the ground without a sound. But she'd not even taken a dozen strides when a figure rose out of the scrub beside her, grasping her by the arm, and pulling her down.

Tadpole yelped. There in the thick undergrowth, his eyes blazing, was Nutcracker.

Tadpole trudged behind the guard along the ridge, back to the sett. When they were almost at the crevice, Nutcracker dropped down and gestured for her to do the same. Tadpole lowered herself on to grey stone.

Down by Wild Cat Rock, a different group of humans stumbled along the path, their arms flailing. Soon Tadpole could no longer hear their worried babbling. They were gone and would probably never return to the mountain. Nutcracker allowed himself a little chuckle of satisfaction. Moments later, Backfire and Eggnog slipped out from behind a boulder before doubling back and striding up the slope towards home.

Nutcracker got to his feet. "Come on, youngling," he muttered.

It was Deadend the gatekeeper who brought Tadpole to see the silverback, her legs trembling as she walked. They found Rainstorm surrounded by lanterns, sitting as still as a stone, Hindsight as ever by his side. Handmade *(she who creates pretty things)* stood behind an easel, making delicate sweeps on a piece of silver bark with etching charcoal. Tadpole could see a likeness of Rainstorm on the bark, though it was still very rough.

Handmade completed a few more scratches and stopped. "Shall we continue later?"

Rainstorm gave the artist a nod. "It's for the silverback wall," he explained as Handmade left the room.

Tadpole swallowed, the inside of her mouth dry and sour.

"This one was up on the surface without permission," said Deadend. "I've already sent for her mother."

"And here she is now," said Rainstorm as Shipshape swept into the cave.

Tadpole avoided her mum's baffled stare.

"What's this about?" asked Shipshape. "Tadpole?"

"The youngling decided to sneak out," said Rainstorm. "Against my orders."

"And while she was meant to be painting the tunnels ready for the Collective," added Hindsight.

"Is this true?" Shipshape squinted at Tadpole.

Tadpole hurriedly thought up a story, her eyes beginning to fill. "I saw a group of Greybeards going out and wanted to see what was going on. I was curious."

"You had no right to, Tadpole," said Shipshape.

Tadpole wiped her eyes with the back of her hand. "But Mum, I saw them Murmuring," she whispered.

"Murmuring!"

"I watched two humans being chased off the mountain, and then another group too."

Shipshape turned to Rainstorm. "Murmuring?"

Rainstorm looked a little uncomfortable. "Yes," he answered at last. "In the interests of safety, I have ordered teams of Murmurers to sweep the mountain."

"Murmuring?" said Shipshape again. "But we Greybeards haven't Murmured in cycles. I thought we'd moved on from those dark times."

"We've never had the Collective visit us before either," answered Rainstorm. "*Wise is the deer who bellows at the skulking stoat.*"

"True, true," agreed Hindsight. "We can't have humans threatening the Gathering, Shipshape."

"Should we have to hide underground only to emerge fearful and in secret the way we do now? Or should we run on the peaks like we used to?" Rainstorm gestured at the wall of silverbacks.

"All we've done is set up a protective boundary – to keep the humans away from our peak," said Hindsight. "And there's nothing in the slab laws that says we are not permitted to do so. The humans can choose another place to trample all over and leave their muck."

"We share this Earth," said Shipshape. "We should learn to live alongside each other. Not build barriers."

"I'm sorry, but things are different now." Rainstorm smoothed the sash on his chest. "And that's all there is to it."

Shipshape's head dropped. "I can see that," she said at last.

Tadpole felt rotten. Shipshape didn't have a smile on her face like the one in the portrait now.

Rainstorm gave Tadpole a cold glare. "Your behaviour leaves a lot to be desired, youngling. Out of respect for your parents, I will give you another chance to prove that you can be a good Greybeard – I trust you will see that she obeys this time, Shipshape?"

Shipshape nodded. "I will."

"Now off you go, and paint that tunnel," said Hindsight.

★

Tadpole found her paintpot and ladder where she'd left them, and soon her paintbrush swung back and forth over the ceiling, and little white drops scattered to the floor once more. She thought about the hut, the *specktakulls*, rescuing Hen-ree, sneaking out to get the map, her mum. The terrible Murmuring.

What a few moons it had been. Now everything seemed hugely different. "But isn't that what you wanted – a different life?" she muttered, her voice heavy with scorn.

★

Hi love,

Hope things are going well at Halbrook. Better than they are here at any rate. The other day, Karman marched off into the countryside. He said he wanted to be alone.

We haven't seen him for days and I'm getting worried, though Dad says he's probably fine. To make things worse, he's taken his manuscript with him, so there's no way we can work on it. Beginning to wonder if we're going to pull this book off at all.

But you don't want to hear all about that. Tell us your news. We haven't heard much. Please write when you can. Would be good to chat, but we rarely get into the village, and don't seem to be online at the same times.

Love Mum

"Spicy OK?" asked Murray, interrupting.

"Hmm?" Henry looked up from his phone.

"Your noodles?" Murray pointed at the bowls sitting on his desk.

"Oh, right," said Henry. "Yes please." Murray rummaged in the drawer below his bed and found a packet. "Thanks for this, Murray. Dinner was awful."

"Brussel sprouts and grey mince." Murray gave a shiver. "The worst."

Henry laughed. "Ever had chicken's feet? It's just loads of tiny bones."

When the kettle boiled, Murray filled Henry's bowl and handed it to him. "That's nothing. I had this special sausage dish on holiday once. Looked all right at the start, but once you cut into it chopped-up guts spilled all over the plate."

"A sausage made from guts?"

"Yep. You should have smelled it!" Murray wrinkled his nose. "Even though I was gagging, Dad made me eat the whole thing."

Henry gave his noodles a stir. "Harsh."

Murray sighed. "Dad's kind of strict. Always on about me keeping up the Roth name."

"Not sure the Wetwoods have much of a name."

"Well, you should have met my grandfather, Remus. When my dad was a kid, he used to make him choose the chicken for dinner and…" Murray drew a finger across his throat. He smiled. "Still fancy coming to stay this weekend?"

"As long as I don't have to choose a chicken – or eat its feet."

Murray chuckled. "Nah. Nothing like that. I'll text Dad."

The following moon, having finished painting the entrance tunnel, Tadpole was ordered by Hindsight to the new landing dock down in the water channel – where the Collective ambassadors would soon arrive.

"Handmade has drawn a new Collective sign. You're to fill it in with paint," said the Guardian.

"Of course, Hindsight," said Tadpole, noticing how grumpy the elder had got since becoming Guardian.

Tadpole made her way down to the waterhole with her pot and brush. Her dad and his team were still hard at work, running buckets, turning the waterwheel, shaking boxes. Waterworks looked worried. His beloved Shadowspring was growing weaker by the moon. Tadpole gave him a wave and a smile and carried on to the far end of the cavern. She passed Crewcut on one of the shaking frames, pushing and pulling.

"Hey," said Crewcut over the sloshing of the water and the rolling of the gravel. "Come to give me a hand?"

"Afraid not." Tadpole held up her paintpot.

"Rather you than me," Crewcut puffed. "Give me Shadowspring any moon."

"You really like doing all this, don't you, Crewcut?" Tadpole gestured at the giant cavern and the teams of yeti bustling about.

"Oh yes," Crewcut beamed. "Of course, it can get a little dull sometimes, but then I think of all the things that enjoy our clean water. Makes it totally worth it."

Tadpole thought about this for a moment. She had never looked at Shadowspring that way. Perhaps Crewcut was right. It wasn't just about the Greybeards, it was about others: the trees, the birds, the animals.

"Well, I'd better get started," she said, carrying on down the bank of the waterway and into the darkened tunnel.

Inside the large passageway, the water channel branched off. One stream carried on deep into the Earth, the waterway that connected the sett to the Collective. The other flowed out on to the mountainside to feed the valley.

A new dock had been built of tree trunks, ready for the canoes of the ambassadors. Tadpole stepped out on to it, testing the planks. Above the dock, Handmade had etched a symbol into the rock wall lit up by firefly lanterns: a circle, like the world itself, and in the middle was a footprint. A large sole and four enormous toes. The sign of the International Yeti Collective.

Tadpole laid out her groundsheet, put down her paintpot and dipped in her brush, careful not to let any drops fall. She knew that just a single drop of paint in the channel could spoil a whole lot of water. Tadpole started with the sole of the foot, making sure she stayed within the lines.

Until recently, she hadn't even known that the waterways still connected all the yeti setts across the world. What was it like, she wondered, flowing with the current, knowing that above your head mountains and oceans passed by? Stepping out into a different land. A place where no one knew who you were.

Tadpole had just finished the sole and one of the toes when, all of a sudden, the ground began to shake. A deep rumble from below. Ripples shook the water's surface.

"Trembles!" gasped Tadpole, covering her head, trying to steady her feet.

Then, before she had time to panic, the trembling stopped and all was quiet. Tadpole left her pot and brush and ran out of the tunnel. Work in the waterhole had come to a stop. The Greybeards downed tools and burbled to each other in worried bursts.

Tadpole went over to join her dad. "Another one!"

"They seem to be getting worse," said Waterworks. "Are you OK?"

Tadpole stared down at the pool of water. "Is it my imagination or did the water level just drop again?"

Waterworks' eyes widened. "Grab the rope."

Tadpole went to the equipment store and came back with the measuring rope, dropping it in as fast as she could. She started to count aloud, stopping when she reached ten.

"Ten knots!" gasped Waterworks. "It was fourteen this morning!"

"Do these trembles have anything to do with it?"

"I wish I knew." Waterworks scratched his head. "It gets worse and worse. I've never known anything like it – and that's with us working as fast as we can." He gestured at the Greybeards who were back pushing and pulling the shaking boxes, the water carriers jogging with their buckets. "As if we didn't already have enough to worry about."

Tadpole eyed the giant sand timer on the wall of the cave. "Better get back to my paintbrush." It was going to be a long moon.

★

Far below the ground, paddling along the Great North Passage, Dunkk *(she who dips biscuits)* of the Makimaki felt the bottom of the canoe scrape against a rock. "There it is again!"

"I felt it too," said Songg *(he with tuneful voice)*. He reached his paddle down as far as he could into the stream and found the bottom. "The closer we get to the Greybeards, the lower the water is getting, no question."

"If it keeps dropping, we could have trouble reaching them at all."

"Not to mention getting back to our sett," said Songg.

Dunkk considered this for a time. "Let's keep going," she decided.

★

Leeke *(she who smells pleasingly like onions)* of the Mande Barung stood on the rocky shelf of a landing spot and took another mouthful of mango cricket, munching as she looked down at the waterway. She cleared her throat. "*Half a loaf is better than no bread.*"

"I suppose," said Twangg *(she who strums instruments)*.

"So what do we do?" asked Plott *(he who schemes)*.

"The water in these passageways of ours has flowed since the Earth began," said Leeke. "And it will flow long after we're gone. But let's ask Flittermouse to fly ahead as a precaution."

Leeke turned to the bat hanging from her shoulder, fast asleep, and tickled her under the chin. Flittermouse popped her little head out from behind her wings and listened to Leeke's instructions.

With a yawn and a squeak, she unfurled her wings and flapped off down the tunnel.

★

Bluntt *(he with coarse tongue)* paced the landing spot, staring at the canoe, while the other Yeren stretched their stiff legs. "We're going to have to leave the seeds behind." He gestured at the wooden box strapped to the middle of the boat.

"Not the seeds," said Trampp *(she who likes to walk far)*.

"I see no other way. If we keep hitting the bottom, we're in danger of holing."

Frostt *(he of chilly disposition)* kneeled down and felt the fabric stretched over the frame of the boat. "He's right. One jagged rock and we're done."

"Give us a hand then," Trampp sighed.

The Yeren kneeled on the bank and, straining together, they lifted the box and placed it in the corner of the cavern, underneath the Collective sign etched into the wall.

"Such a shame," said Bluntt. "We didn't even get a chance to spread them."

"At least we tried," said Frostt as the Yeren climbed back into their boat.

★

Not far behind them, the Orang Pendek were facing their own troubles. "Piled up high like a beehive?" asked Strut. He grabbed a handful of his long, lustrous hair and twirled it into a mound on the top of his head.

"That certainly adds a bit of height," Mould panted, his arms pumping.

"Or a braid sitting on either side of my head like this?" The Orang Pendek made the braids in a flash and placed them over his ears like two clamshells.

"That's certainly different," said Mould.

"So many choices."

"They all look good."

"*But if hair is worth doing it's worth doing well.*"

"Any chance you could give me a hand?" said Mould.

★

The mood on board the Mountain Yeti boat had not improved. "Not only are we lower, but we're getting slower," grumbled Nagg.

"We're paddling as hard as we can," Tick puffed. "But, ever since we entered the channel towards the Greybeards, the current just isn't as strong as before."

"It's as if the water's running out." Nagg peered over the side of the boat.

"How is that even possible?" asked Tick.

"Humans," grumbled Nagg.

"Come on, Nagg, you can't blame them for everything," said Plumm.

"Humans," repeated the elder, leaning back and closing his eyes.

Tick gazed at the stream, willing it to rise. He hoped the other ambassadors weren't struggling too. So much depended on this Gathering. It would take a strong Collective will to go against the tide, to bring the humans back into the fold – the way it had been right at the beginning, in the time of Earth Mother. Yeti had forgotten that once there weren't just nineteen setts: there were twenty.

When Henry and Murray arrived at Roth Manor on Friday, they found Murray's father in the front grounds in a cap and boots, along with the men Henry had seen in the barn at school, out of their suits and each with a rifle in their hands. At the far end of the rolling lawn stood several cardboard targets. Even at this distance, Henry could see that they had been ripped to shreds. A groundskeeper was busy taking them down.

"Still time for you to have a go if you like," said Roth, coming over to greet them.

"You know how I feel about guns, Dad," said Murray.

"Worth a try." Roth gave him a big hug, clapping him warmly on the back.

"Hello, Mr Roth," said Henry.

"Nice to see you." Murray's dad offered him his rifle.

"No thanks, Mr Roth."

"Another conscientious objector," said Roth, disappointed. "These are my friends, Mr Jarvis and Mr MacNeil."

Henry shook their hands, wincing as both men took it upon themselves to crush his fingers. With his flattened ears and bent nose, Jarvis wouldn't have looked out of place in a boxing ring. MacNeil towered over everyone else, thin and sour.

Roth's face brightened. "Guess what, Murray, the razorbacks arrived earlier this week! Come and see."

"I think we'll just go up to my room," said Murray.

"Don't be silly – it'll be exciting for Henry. They're over by the stables." Roth and the others gave their guns to the groundskeeper and set off towards the back of the house.

"What are razorbacks?" asked Henry.

"I'm not sure you really want to know," said Murray.

They crossed a cobbled yard towards some barns. Roth led them to a pen tucked away at the back, a muddy yard ringed by a steel fence. Behind the barricade, breathing heavily as they rooted around in the dirt, were a pair of wild boars. Thick, long hair covered the animals, rising to a crest along the ridge of their backs. Sharp tusks stuck out from their lower jaws, reaching above their upper lips like curved blades. They were the biggest pigs Henry had ever seen, their eyes cold and full of menace.

"Razorbacks," said Roth. "I ordered them specially at

Jarvis's suggestion."

Jarvis gave a slow nod.

"What for?" asked Henry.

"Did you know that wild boars like this sometimes hunt down small animals to eat?" said Jarvis.

"No."

"Neither did I," admitted Roth.

Jarvis grinned. "Well, this breed are real carnivores. They've also been trained to track prey."

One of the boars plodded through the sludge towards Henry, grunting. Using its front trotters, it raised itself up against the fence, jaws grinding, slobber dripping down the sides of its mouth.

Henry flinched and stepped back. "You can do that?"

"Red deer, stag, foxes – you name it, these boars will find it," added MacNeil. "Amazing, isn't it?"

"Yes," said Henry, not sure what to say.

In the pen, the boar butted heads, squealing and snorting.

"I'm telling you, Roth, they're going to be even better than dogs," said Jarvis. "Once they get a sniff of something, they don't give up."

"Can't wait to give them their first run-out," said Roth.

"Let's go up to my room." Murray tugged on Henry's arm.

"I'll call you down for dinner." Roth leaned over and

patted one of the boars on the head.

Murray led Henry through the grand entrance hall. The walls of the hall rose up to a ceiling entirely covered with an elaborate painting, like a church roof. There were gold frames on the walls, each one holding a glowering portrait. Henry thought about the tiny hallway of his family flat in London. "Wow."

"Looks like it's really posh, right?" Murray sniffed.

"Like something off TV," Henry agreed.

"Wait. You haven't seen it all." Murray skipped up the grand staircase at the far end, and down a long hallway lined with doorway after doorway, floorboards creaking under their feet.

Henry gazed down the corridor in both directions. It seemed never-ending. "How many rooms are there?"

"Loads," said Murray, stopping. "Choose a door."

Henry shrugged and picked the one nearest to them, turning the brass handle and pushing it open. Inside, the room was bare. Wallpaper drooped from the walls like peeled banana skin. On one wall, the plaster had come away altogether, revealing rows of wooden slats. The chunks of plaster still sat on the floorboards where they had fallen. "What happened in here?"

Without answering, Murray pulled the door shut and crossed the hallway, opening another. It too was bleak and smelled of mould. "Lots of rooms are like this."

Henry wrinkled his nose. "How come?"

"We can't afford to keep it up. The house has been slowly turning into a ruin. Whatever you do, don't let on I showed you."

"I won't."

"Anyway, Dad reckons he's going to have enough money to fix it soon."

"That's good, right?"

"I guess so. But I'm not sure why we need a house this big. And not if it means he's partners with Jarvis and MacNeil. They're a bit off. Hope they're not staying for dinner." Henry thought back to the barn, the way he'd heard them all arguing with Mr Dossit.

Murray carried on and stopped at a door at the end of the hallway. "My room's a bit better." He leaned into the heavy door.

Murray was right – his room fitted the part of a stately home. High ceiling, the walls covered in wood panels. There was a soft red carpet and a marble fireplace. At one end was a massive four-poster bed, with carved pillars that rose up to the ceiling. But Henry thought it looked more like an expensive hotel room than a kid's bedroom.

He dumped his bag on the spare bed in the corner.

"But where's all *your* stuff?"

Murray went over and opened a door almost hidden in the panelling. Inside was a cupboard of clothes, toys and gadgets. "Dad has rules about tidiness."

Henry spotted shelves full of paint bottles and brushes. "Are those all your art things?"

Murray took down a canvas to show him. It was a painting of a family of three standing in front of Roth Manor, the sky blue and cheerful above their heads.

"Is that your mum?" For the first time, Henry realized he'd never heard Murray talk about her before.

"She lives in Spain," said Murray.

"Oh," said Henry.

"I don't use my paints all that much at home." Murray slipped the canvas back. "Do your parents always tell you what you should do?"

Henry shrugged. "They say I should try to do what makes me happy."

"Lucky you." Murray checked his watch. "We still have some time before dinner," he said, changing the subject. "How about you show me Vault and Serpent properly? Did you bring your cards?"

Henry grinned. "See, I told you it would grow on you."

★

It was just the three of them at dinner – lasagne, washed down with more Pure Origins water. Henry was about to refuse the bottled water, but didn't want to seem rude to his host. When they finished, Murray's dad suggested the boys light a fire in the library, which sounded like a great idea. Some of the rooms in Murray's house were colder than it was outside.

Henry had never lit a fire before, so Murray showed him how to build a little pyre with kindling and newspaper. He let Henry light the match and get the fire going and, as it burned, they fed split logs into the flames, then settled into the high back of the sofa.

Henry and Murray watched the blaze, warming their hands.

"We used to do this all the time – sit by the fire," said Murray, breaking the quiet. "Before Mum and Dad split up."

"What happened?"

"They argued all the time, even about really small stuff. It wasn't much fun. I don't blame Mum for taking time away – really I don't," said Murray. "They say it's only a trial separation, but it's been ages."

Henry thought about his own family. Dad serving up his one pasta dish for dinner, squeezed together, laughing and chatting, round their small dinner table. Mum asking Dad what his secret ingredient in the sauce was, even though she'd had it a hundred times. "You never know, Murray, your parents could get back together," he said brightly.

"Hope so," said Murray.

Henry looked over at his friend. It had been brave to share all that. He made up his mind. "Murray, if I tell you something, will you promise to keep it to yourself?"

Murray looked a little surprised. "Of course. What?"

"You can't tell anyone. Especially not your dad. Swear."

Murray made a cross sign over his heart.

Henry stared back at the fire for a moment, the crackling of the wood disrupting the silence of the library. "Remember on the day of the tramp. How I came back to school late?"

Murray gave a slow nod.

"Well, it wasn't just that I tripped and fell," Henry whispered. "It was because I met something in the woods."

Murray looked puzzled. "What do you mean?"

"You *know* what I mean."

"No, I don't."

"You've even painted one."

Murray thought for a moment. His eyes widened. "You don't mean…"

"Yes."

"A Grey…"

"Yes."

"Flippin' heck," said Murray. "No way. For real?"

"For real."

In whispers, Henry told Murray everything he knew

about Tadpole. How she rescued him from the fall and spoke to him. About her curious eyes, the terrible stink. Henry described finding the secret hollow again, about Budge, and how it was once the home of Hazel Halbrook – the ex-headmistress of their school. While the two of them talked, Henry found himself relieved to share the secret with someone: it had filled him to bursting.

Murray listened with his mouth open. "I still can't believe it," he said.

Henry held out his phone. He scrolled through to the murky shape of Tadpole in the trees. "Believe it now?"

Murray took the phone from Henry and his bottom jaw began to sag. They sat in silence and stared at the picture with just the roaring fire, the pop and crack of firewood, and the secret of all secrets. Now *their* secret.

"Greybeard!" A sudden voice behind them made them both yelp.

Henry spun round to see Roth leaning over the back of the sofa, holding two steaming mugs and peering down at the phone in Murray's hands. How long had he been standing there? Roth's gaze was glued to the screen.

Henry grabbed the phone from Murray and turned it off.

"Dad!" Murray cried. "We didn't hear you come in."

"The photo – Henry, the photo!" said Roth. "Greybeard!"

"It's nothing," Henry blurted.

"Did you take it on the school hike?" Roth gasped.

Henry shook his head.

"That photo was taken in the woods near here, wasn't it? Near the track." Roth's eyes glistened.

"It's not a Greybeard." Henry could feel his face reddening. "It was just a shadow. Out on the tramp."

"Then show me again," said Roth. Henry didn't budge, but it didn't seem to matter to Roth. "Finally, after all these years! Have you any idea what this means? An actual sighting!"

Henry's heart began to race. He scrambled for words. "It was just a funny-looking shadow."

"That photo is no shadow," said Roth. "You know it and I know it. What a beast!" He put the mugs on the side table. "There's something I need to show you. You can have the hot chocolate later."

Henry gave Murray an alarmed look as Roth shepherded them out of the library and through the great hall to a doorway at the far end. With a flourish, he threw the door open.

"Look at that!"

Henry stood and gawked. Dozens of animal heads covered the walls: deer with towering curled antlers; others with horns so long and sharp they were like daggers; snow-white mountain hares and giant moose. On the floor stood a wild cat, hissing. Birds hung by wires from the ceiling. Everything in here had once been breathing, had once been alive.

Henry stumbled through the room in a daze. Trapped behind glass, a buffalo with curved horns bellowed in terror as a lion sank its teeth into its neck, one paw raking the skin on its nose, the other its back. The wrinkle of anger in the lion's muzzle was so convincing that Henry felt his hand reaching for his own throat.

"The best piece in the room, isn't it?" said Roth. "My father shot them both at a waterhole in Africa. Though not at the same time, of course. He had them arranged like that. What a magnificent trophy."

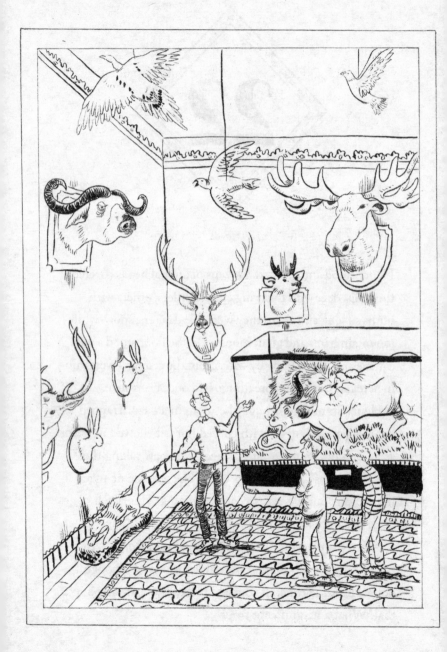

Henry felt numb.

"Everything in here was shot by a Roth. Grandfather took care of plenty, Dad as well," said Roth.

"And you, Mr Roth?" asked Henry.

Roth took him over to an enormous set of antlers. "How about that twenty-pointer? Bagged him years ago with Dad. Glorious animal."

"*Was* a glorious animal," mumbled Murray.

"Still waiting for Murray to get his first."

Murray looked at the floor.

"And big game is what I want to talk to you about." Roth examined Henry, craning his long neck.

Henry felt his breath catch in his throat. "I don't understand, Mr Roth."

"Tell me about your Greybeard. You got right up close to it. Then you took a photo."

"There was no Greybeard. Just mist," Henry stammered.

"Just mist?" Roth chuckled. "Come on – I know what I saw! I can see by your face you're not telling me everything."

Henry squirmed but said nothing. He shot a pleading look at Murray, but Murray still had his eyes on his shoes.

"Come and look at this." Roth took Henry's arm and steered him over to a glass case on the other side of the trophy room. The case was quite a bit taller and wider than Henry, and empty. On it was a brass nameplate that read *Greybeard.* "My grandfather had this case specially built, but he never could fill it. Dad neither. Now tell me, Henry: the creature you saw, would it fit in this case, or do I need to get a bigger one?"

Henry swallowed. He pictured Tadpole – frozen, lifeless – inside the glass prison. He turned away. "I don't know, Mr Roth."

Roth ran his fingers over the nameplate. "Listen, Henry, for ages people have come to these ranges, searching for the Greybeards, with nothing but a few shadows and stories to show for it. Dad and Grandfather would have jumped at the chance of hunting one down. But they were looking in the wrong place all those years, the wrong mountains. Then you – at Halbrook barely a few days – get that photo in the woods. I can hardly believe it."

"It wasn't like that."

"I just want to know what you saw, Henry," Roth pleaded. "How many hands was it at the shoulder? Was it on two legs or on all fours? I need to know what I'm up against."

Henry tried to keep his voice from breaking. "There was nothing there," he insisted.

Roth scrutinized Henry with bulging eyes. "If I was the one to help Jarvis and MacNeil hunt down a Greybeard… What if we could even capture it alive? It would be worth a fortune to us!"

"It was just shadows." Henry knew he didn't sound convincing.

"Leave him alone, please, Dad," Murray whispered finally.

Roth's eyes glittered. "Well, whether you help us or not, thanks to you I know a Greybeard is out there, and now I also know where to look. Why, there could be a whole herd of them!" He went over to his gun cabinet. "I'll use the variable scope and the electronic hunting muffs!" He pointed to a pair of bright red earmuffs.

"Electronic muffs?" said Murray.

"The latest thing. They let hunters speak to each other, but block out sounds like gunshots. Jarvis and MacNeil told me about them – I bought you a pair too." Roth clapped his hands. "Of course! The razorbacks! Their first run out!"

Henry hung his head.

"I suppose there's no chance you'll let me have another look at that photo, is there?" asked Roth.

"It was just shadows."

"Never mind. I know where the track to Ben Bell cuts above the woods. We'll start there, and then we'll let the razorbacks do their thing. There's bound to be fresh scent. Got to be. I'm off to call the others." Roth hurried to the door. "Expect an early start, boys!"

"I'm sorry, Henry," said Murray when Roth had left. "Dad doesn't know when to let things go."

"This is all my fault," Henry groaned. "Me and that stupid photo. And now your dad and his friends will hunt Tadpole down. How long do you think it will take others to come? The entire world will be out looking for the Greybeards. What have I done?"

"It isn't your fault."

"Yes, it is. Me and my big mouth."

Murray let out a long breath. "Well, I don't see what we can do about it."

"Is there any chance your dad and the others won't bother?"

"Look around you." Murray gestured at the trophy cabinets. "It's what Roths do."

23

Up in Murray's room, Henry paced from the bed to the window, then back to the bed. He couldn't sit still. "Somehow I have to tell Tadpole and her friends to hide. They must stay off the mountain – at least until we can somehow get your dad and the others to give up."

"How do you plan on doing that? Do you even know where to find these Greybeards?" asked Murray.

"Haven't got a clue." Henry sighed. Then he thought of the last time he met Tadpole. "There is the bothy."

"What was it called again?"

"Budge. But the chances are probably nil. Tadpole said she really wasn't supposed to be there."

"Anything else?" asked Murray.

Henry shook his head. He went over to the window. Outside, he could see trees at the far end of the grounds in the last of the day's light. "Those woods stretch all the way

181

to school, right? Do you think I could get to Budge from here?"

"How could you possibly find the bothy in there?" Murray gestured at the gloomy woods.

His friend was right. It was one thing on a sunny afternoon, another in darkness. Were there any landmarks that could help him? Henry thought back to the first time he'd found his way to the hut. What about the brook? "Let's say I go in far enough, and I head towards the school, somewhere in the middle of the woods I'd run across the stream, right?"

"And?"

"Well, the brook runs right near the ring of stones. I followed it last time. If I found the stream again, I'm fairly sure it would lead me to the secret hollow," said Henry.

"Sure, or fairly sure?"

Henry could only shrug.

"I still think you're daft. Believe me, I don't want to see Dad's glass case filled any more than you do," said Murray, "but the woods – at night?"

"Can you think of another way?" Henry sighed. Murray didn't have anything to say. "What choice do I have? I don't want to go out there either, but I have to."

Murray nodded. "Then you'll need some gear." He opened his cupboard and found a pair of massive torches, turning them on to test the beam. He handed one to

Henry. Then in a drawer he found some walkie-talkies. "They're good ones. Like the army use. Signal travels for miles. We can use them to stay in touch – in case we split up."

"We?"

"I'm not letting you go on your own."

Henry shook his head. "No, you have to stay here and cover for me. If we both go, there's a bigger chance of being found out."

"All by yourself? Are you serious?"

"Think about it. We need someone to keep an eye on things back here – you can let me know what's going on with the handset. Be a spy – like James Bond."

Murray considered this for a moment. "But as soon as you get to the woods turn your handset on – OK?"

"Will do," said Henry. "When I'm done, I'll come straight back. As quick as I can."

He grabbed his bag and tossed out the contents. Of the things he'd brought, he decided to keep the notebook and pencils, and put them back into the bag along with both the torches – just in case one died.

Murray turned on his walkie-talkie and pressed the talk button. "Testing, testing."

Henry gave him a thumbs up and put his walkie-talkie in the chest pocket of his jacket. "All right, ready to go."

"No, we need to wait until Dad's gone to sleep. Can't

risk him catching you." Murray let out a sigh. "I've never done anything like this before. He'll blow his lid if he finds out."

"Thanks for helping me, Murray."

"Let's go to bed, and I'll set my alarm."

"There's no chance of me going to sleep," Henry said. All the same, he left his gear in a tidy pile, slipped off his shoes and climbed under the duvet fully clothed.

He checked his phone.

Hey,

Karman came back from his walk, and when Dad asked when we could get back to work on the book, he just laughed.

He says he's decided to write off one of the main characters altogether and take the book in a new direction. Apparently, communing with nature has changed his whole way of thinking. He's shut himself in his bedroom with the manuscript. Not sure just what we're going to do.

What's your news?

If only I dared tell you, Henry thought. It would have to wait.

Then Murray turned off the lights. "Goodnight."

★

The next thing Henry knew, Murray was shaking him by the shoulder. "Good thing I set the alarm, eh?"

When Henry was ready, Murray opened his bedroom door and stuck his head out into the dark corridor. "Come with me," he whispered. "We'll use the back stairs."

The two boys took the tiny, winding staircase at the back of Roth Manor. With the groan of each floorboard, and the hollow thud coming from the steps, Henry was certain there would be a sudden flood of light and Murray's dad would appear. But they were soon standing on the stone kitchen floor. Then Murray unlocked the door and they slipped out into the night.

"Are you still sure you want to do this?" Murray whispered.

"I'm not sure at all," said Henry. "But I'm going to anyway."

"OK, you go to the hut and, if that Greybeard isn't there, you come right back. Anything happens, you leg it."

"Got it."

"I'll be with you on the walkie-talkie the whole way."

The two friends gave each other an awkward hug and then Henry jogged round to the trees fringing the front lawn and followed them into the woods. If Li and David could see him now! Pushing on into a dark wood, on his own. Seeking out a legendary creature to spoil a hunt. But this wasn't a simple roll of the dice in one of their games.

Though the moon hadn't reached its peak, cool light streamed through the trees, casting long shadows over the forest floor. Far above Henry's head, the trees groaned to each other in the wind. Each crunching twig under his boots sounded like a gunshot, his breath rasping and loud. It took all his will not to turn round and run back to the manor.

A crackle came from inside his jacket, making Henry jump, and then Murray's voice. "Testing, testing. Are you receiving? Over."

Henry took out the walkie-talkie. "Loud and clear. See you soon. Over and out." In the still of the woods, it sounded like he was shouting. He scanned the darkness for wild-animal eyes, relieved that he didn't see any.

24

Henry pushed deep into the woods until he met the stream. The water seemed to have almost vanished in places, leaving little more than a trickle. But, with the moonlight and his torch, Henry now had a route. In his head, he could see Roth out on the hunt in these woods, red earmuffs on, rifle in hand, MacNeil and Jarvis by his side. Henry pictured the boars snarling, razor-sharp tusks flashing. He saw Greybeards fleeing for cover.

Please be at the hut, Tadpole, thought Henry. He didn't have a plan B.

Henry picked up the pace when he caught sight of the boulders in his torchlight. He was just starting to doubt he would reach the hollow at all when he found the gap in the stones, exploring it with the beam to make sure there were no night visitors, before pushing in. Henry took the steps one at a time. Stopping, listening. Then he slipped into the clearing. Was Tadpole there? A quick look around told Henry he was alone.

He held his breath, then gently pushed the door to Budge open and swept the beam round the little bothy. The hut was exactly as he'd left it. The books, the mirror, the pot-bellied stove, the ladder up to the loft. A museum. He took a deep sniff, but could only detect a hint of farmyard smell. He guessed Tadpole hadn't been back since the last time. She obviously wasn't here. Henry felt hollow.

So now what? he wondered. *Do I wait? Do I go back to Roth Manor? Or do I dare keep trying to find her?*

He thought back to the time they met. When he asked Tadpole about her home, she'd shaken her head and changed the subject. Her home was a secret. But still, she'd come to the bothy at least twice. The time she'd stopped him from falling, and the time she'd surprised him at the doorway to Budge.

Henry went over to the bookshelves and found Tadpole's handprint still visible in the dust. Last time he had been standing right there, holding the pendant in his hand, the one he'd found sitting on the shelf. She had taken a risk to come to Budge to get that pendant back. But why?

Henry remembered he'd taken a photo of it. He felt around in his jeans for his phone, and scrolled through to the gallery, his face lit by the blue glow. He found the one of the markings on the back of Tadpole's pendant. Henry dragged the photo until the pattern of symbols filled the whole screen.

He traced the symbols with his finger. They reminded him of something – history class, and the Roman maps. The symbols – they were like something off a chart!

Now the patterns started to make sense. If he was looking at it correctly, there appeared to be a peak, a forest, a circle of stones and a hut with a pointed roof. Circle of stones. The hut – with a trail leading from the front door. Was this map to help Tadpole find the bothy?

Henry noticed a line on the map that could be the path that led to Ben Bell. The starting point of the map, marked with a squiggle, was on the next mountain over, above two semi-circular shapes he guessed were the rocky domes he'd noticed on the tramp. If that was the starting point, was there a small chance it was where the Greybeards lived? If he was right, it gave him a way to find Tadpole.

Henry got out his notebook and pencil. Using the photo on the screen, he began to copy out a larger version of the map – taking his time to make sure he'd put all the symbols in the right place. Then he found his walkie-talkie and pressed the talk button. "Murray, are you there?"

There was a hiss of white noise and then a squelch.

"Receiving you. Where are you?"

"At the hut. She's not here."

"You gave it your best. You'd better come back then."

"No, I'm going to try and find her on the mountain."

"What? No way, Henry, that's mad," squawked Murray.

Henry glanced out of the window at the sky. "There's a bright moon. Let's hope it stays that way. If it looks hopeless, I'll come back down. Don't worry, I'll stay in touch. Over."

Rather than carry on through the woods towards Halbrook and then backtrack in the direction of Ben Bell, Henry decided it would be quicker to leave level ground and head up the slope to meet the tramping trail. He would leave the dark woods, the branches blocking out the sky, and get out on to the hillside to find his bearings. Then, as long as the sky was cloudless, and the moonlight stayed strong, he might be able to set a good pace.

Henry left the hollow by the stairs, doubled back and began climbing the slope. To push himself up the incline, he dug his shoes into the soft dirt, grabbing hold of ferns. More than once he slipped, dropping down to his knees, before pushing himself back up and carrying on, struggling his way past thick tree trunks.

Now the woodland ahead of him began to thin out, and then Henry caught sight of the thin, pale scar of the trail cut into the side of the hill. With a final heave, he got himself up on to the ridge.

Free of the canopy, he gazed at the ranges spread out around him in the moonlight, layer after layer like the painted set of a stage play, waiting for giant actors to appear from the wings. The trees obstructed the valley, but Henry knew that the lights of Halbrook lay just on the other side of the woods, the boys asleep in their rooms. What would Mr Dossit say if he could see him now? Henry didn't dare imagine.

He took another look at the map he'd copied. He'd stick to the trail that led towards Ben Bell, then leave the path and strike out through the scrub for the rounded domes of grey stone. From there, he'd change direction and head for the spot marked with the squiggle. Remembering Murray's advice, he took the walkie-talkie out of his pocket.

"I've reached the trail, heading up the hill now. Speak soon."

"Leave the handset on, OK?"

Henry put the walkie-talkie in his pocket and carried on along the trail. With the handset on in his jacket, it was as if Murray was with him. Henry didn't think he could do this on his own.

25

It was some time later, after Henry had left the path, that something moved in the tussocks of grass, making him jump. He scanned the hillside in the moonlight, finding nothing at first, but then in the beam of his torch he saw it again. A small animal, low to the ground. A mountain hare. The hare stood still, ears down, its fur brown and grey like the hillside, almost perfectly camouflaged but for the white of its chest showing up in the light.

Now the hare pushed itself upright on its long hind legs and studied him for a time, unafraid, it seemed to Henry. Then it hopped down through the scrub towards him, stopping at a safe distance to watch. Was it the same hare that had been with Tadpole?

"Tadpole," Henry called, his voice sounding foolish out on the deserted hillside. "Tadpole," he said again, doing his best to remember the Greybeard's pronunciation.

The hare studied him, and then it bolted up the hillside, jagging one way then the other in a burst of speed. Henry shifted his bag on his back and set off after it.

★

Tadpole was just settling into her nest when a tap on her foot made her jump. It was Lepus.

"We need to talk," said the hare.

"Lepus, sweet whiskers! How did you even get in here?" gasped Tadpole. "And why is your fur all wet?"

"Never mind that now," Lepus squeaked. "I've been searching for your den. Lucky I can recognize your smell. It's about your friend from the hollow."

"Hen-ree?"

"That's the one. Just seen him."

Tadpole gulped. "Really?"

"He saw me too," said Lepus. "He called out your name – at least it sounded like your name. I'm not that good with human tongue."

"Where?"

"On the slope – heading towards the crevice. He seemed to know what he was looking for too."

Tadpole's heart thumped. "Which crevice?"

"The one that leads to the entrance of your sett, of course." Lepus snorted.

"How did he know how to find it?"

Tadpole reached for her necklace, brushing the smooth clay against her lips while she struggled to find answers. Slowly she glanced down. The pendant map. Down at Hazel's place it had been in Hen-ree's hands.

"Why is he coming at all? What does he want?" Snowdrift materialized, sitting down on the edge of the nest.

Tadpole turned to face him. "That's just what I was wondering."

Lepus stared at her, puzzled. "Who are you talking to?"

"It doesn't matter," said Tadpole. "How far away do you reckon Hen-ree is? We need to stop him."

"Hate to say it but he's probably already near your front door."

"Did you spot any other Greybeards out on the hillside?"

Lepus shook his head. "There wasn't a soul."

"Then let's go there now before he gets us all into trouble." Tadpole picked Lepus up and buried him in the crook of her arm. The hare coughed and spluttered, his eyes watering.

"If it's all the same to you, I'd rather hop."

Tadpole crept out of her room. The living den was empty. Shipshape and Waterworks were fast asleep in their nests. She slipped out of the den door, and strolled down the main tunnel, desperate not to draw attention to the damp hare wriggling under her arm.

★

At first, when Henry saw the crevice caught in the beam of his torch, he didn't think it could possibly be the place. It looked too narrow for one thing, and it didn't appear to go back very far. But then he remembered that the hidden entrance through the rocks to Budge didn't look like much at first either. He decided to investigate.

Henry stopped and listened for any sound of movement. Satisfied he was still alone, he peered in, and saw the fissure curved round, before opening into a wider cave. Henry took a deep breath, flaring his nostrils – and then he smelled it. That same sweaty, mouldy-sock-forgotten-in-the-changing-room kind of smell that hung round Tadpole. This could be the right way after all. And, if he could smell it, it wouldn't be difficult for those boars to follow.

Before he went any further, Henry pressed the talk button on the walkie-talkie. "Are you there, Murray?"

There was a crackle, then, "Loud and clear."

"Found the place. About to go in and look for Tadpole."

"Be super careful, Henry."

"Will do."

Henry shone the torch down the crevice, the beam shaking in his hand. What waited for him at the bottom of the cave? He had a sudden thought. Were all

Greybeards as friendly as Tadpole? Judging by the size of them, they could tear him limb from limb if they wanted to. Henry swallowed. He'd come this far. *This is it*, he told himself. *Probably the most daring thing you've ever done in your whole life.*

He squeezed himself into the crack and pushed on until he entered the cave. He stumbled downwards over the rocky floor, his heart pounding. The Greybeards were close by – he could smell it. How much further did he have the guts to go?

Then he came to a giant boulder that stopped him from going on. Dead end. But something about this stone looked different from the rock walls around it. The edges seemed smoother. Was this a doorway? If so, it was firmly shut. How to open it? Did he even want to?

Henry found a loose stone on the ground and gave it a little tap against the giant boulder, stepping back hurriedly. Nothing. He tapped again, louder this time. Still nothing. "Give it a proper knock," Henry grunted to himself. He brought the rock down against the boulder with a loud CRACK. Then again. And once more.

Silence.

Tadpole got to the entranceway just in time to hear loud knocks – like a stone cracking against the other side of the slab. Deadend was alert in an instant, Toothpick and Nutcracker too. They jumped up from their posts where they'd been dozing.

"What in sweet whiskers is that?" asked Deadend.

Toothpick put her ear against the stone. "Is someone stuck out on the mountain?"

The taps came again.

"Raising the gate," said Nutcracker, grabbing the rope.

★

Henry turned to go back the way he'd come. Then a loud rasping and grinding came from the boulder, making him jump. Suddenly the stone rose up from the floor.

In the beam of light, he saw two hairy arms and, before

he could move, a hand clamped itself over his mouth, stifling his scream. Henry felt coarse fur against his face, and hot, searing breath on the back of his neck. Then he blacked out.

★

"Close it, close it!" shouted Toothpick.

Deadend dropped a figure to the floor as Nutcracker let go of the rope, closing the gate with a thud.

From her hiding place, Tadpole stifled a yelp.

"Sweet whiskers!" Nutcracker shrieked. "A human!"

"Right at our sett door!" gasped Toothpick.

Nutcracker shuffled forwards and peered down. "Is he…?"

Tadpole held her breath.

"He's alive. I think he dumfoozled when I grabbed him," Deadend panted. "I can't believe I touched a human!"

"Should I go and wake Rainstorm?" asked Toothpick.

"As fast as you can – and not a word to anyone else."

Toothpick bowed to him, and then scampered off down the tunnel. Tadpole pressed herself into the shadows. She gave Lepus a wide-eyed look. The hare understood. Not a sound.

Now Hen-ree groaned and began to stir. He reached a hand to his face.

Deadend and Nutcracker both leaped back. "Quick, we need something to tie him up with! Fetch a rope," ordered

Deadend, sending Nutcracker running down the tunnel.

Tadpole shrank back as the guard ran past, slumping to the floor, her head in a tangle. "*What do we do?*" she mouthed to Lepus. She grabbed her pendant.

Snowdrift appeared by her side, leaned in and whispered in her ear. "*Always remember, Tadpole, in life it's not what happens to you, but how you react to it that matters.*" He ran a gentle hand down her cheek. "*You must do what your heart tells you is right.*"

Tadpole nodded. What is right. She needed to rescue Hen-ree.

It didn't take long for Nutcracker to return with a long length of rope – and, before Hen-ree came to his senses, the two Greybeards pulled the sack off his back and tied his hands. Then Toothpick hurried back, Rainstorm at her side.

The silverback staggered against the wall of the cave when he saw Hen-ree lying on the ground.

"Sweet whiskers," he gulped.

Hen-ree rolled round and tried to sit up, and the Greybeards all flinched.

"Toothpick, stand guard – stop anyone from coming near," ordered Rainstorm.

Tadpole curled herself up into a ball as the guard walked right past her and stood facing down the tunnel, blocking the way.

Rainstorm gathered himself. "How did he find his way

down the cavern in the dark?"

Deadend held up a long tube. "He had this lantern on him." He stabbed at the button, sending a beam of light shooting down the tunnel. Tadpole winced and jumped back. Deadend turned the lantern off.

"Devious little beast." Rainstorm wrinkled his nose. "And not even the faintest whiff of scent."

"Horrible," agreed Deadend.

"Were there others?" the silverback asked.

"It looks like he was on his own," said Toothpick.

"But how in Earth Mother's name did he find his way right to our front door?" demanded Rainstorm. He glowered at Hen-ree, who was now fully awake.

Tadpole felt a rush of cold sweep over her body. She pressed her forehead against the stone, as if she might somehow vanish. She could hear Hen-ree sobbing under his breath.

Rainstorm nodded at Hen-ree's sack. "We need to look inside that carry sack – there may be clues."

Deadend picked up the sack with two fingers, keeping it at arm's length as if it was a poisonous adder, and brought it over. Tadpole watched as the gatekeeper opened the bag and began removing the things, ignoring Hen-ree, who still struggled against his ropes.

Deadend pulled out what looked like another lantern, a flask of some kind and a book.

Rainstorm picked up the book and flipped through the pages with his long fingers. When he reached the end, he let out a gasp, the hair on his back rising in a crest. Holding the book open, he showed the other Greybeards the page.

"This looks like a map of the mountains, and the sett is clearly marked!" hissed Rainstorm.

"Just where did he get such a map?"

Tadpole felt sick.

"I do not like this. A human with a map! And what if other humans know of this?" Rainstorm began to pace.

"What shall we do, Rainstorm?" asked Deadend.

"We must protect ourselves. Toothpick and Nutcracker, I want you out on the slopes at once, guarding this side of the mountain. Murmur anything that comes close," Rainstorm ordered. "Deadend, wake the Murmuring squad and send them out on the peaks to defend our sett. But not a word about this human boy to anyone. We don't want to cause a panic."

"Yes, Rainstorm," said the Greybeard.

"But first we will put him and his things in an empty storeroom until we work out what to do with him."

★

Henry lay on the ground, his hands aching from the rope, cold dread running over his body giving him the shivers.

He was in a vast tunnel, the walls smooth and rounded. It headed downwards, then seemed to split into several smaller passages. He felt sick to his stomach and a fresh wave of fear rolled over his chest.

Henry gawked at the giant beasts that stood over him, but didn't dare close his eyes. These Greybeards were far bigger than Tadpole, with huge slabs of muscles below their fur, elaborate moustaches like bicycle handlebars, and beards that reached down over rounded bellies.

He couldn't understand a word of what they were saying, but he could tell they were rattled. Rattled and annoyed. When the Greybeard in charge – Henry guessed the cloth band round his chest meant he was the leader – found the page with the map, Henry could see alarm spread across his face. This wasn't good.

27

Deadend raised the slab, and Toothpick and Nutcracker left the sett in a hurry. With the boulder back in place, Deadend lifted Hen-ree to his feet and, pulling on the rope, led him down the tunnel, stopping now and then to see that it was clear before carrying on. Rainstorm carried Hen-ree's sack over his shoulder, the boy's book in his other hand.

Tadpole shrank back behind the boulder, turning her face as they passed by, then trailed after them, keeping to the shadows.

Rainstorm slid back the bolt on the door and heaved it open. "In there," he ordered. "Throw that human's sack and lantern in too – I don't want anyone coming across it."

Tadpole's heart dropped at the sight of the dark, windowless room. Deadend pushed Hen-ree inside and slammed the door shut. Then the silverback and the gatekeeper strode down the tunnel, Rainstorm gripping Hen-ree's book.

★

Inside the tight space of the storeroom, Henry began to panic. The choking smell and the total darkness were almost unbearable. He felt along the walls for an opening – some way out – but his hands only discovered rock and earth. In his plan, he'd pictured Tadpole greeting him as a friend. Showering him with thanks for risking his life to bring them the warning. But here he was, trapped instead.

★

Making sure the others had gone, Tadpole crept to the storeroom door, Lepus by her side. She was about to slide back the bolt when she took a deep breath and paused. Once she released Hen-ree, she needed to get him back to his home. The entrance to the sett was out of the question and, even if they did manage to sneak out that way, Toothpick and Nutcracker stood guard on the other side.

Tadpole turned to the mountain hare. "Just how *did* you get into our sett, Lepus?"

Lepus looked a little bashful. "I'm not sure you want to know."

"Trust me, I want to know."

"I hopped along the stream and followed it until I

reached your waterhole."

"Shadowspring? How was that even possible?" Tadpole frowned.

"The water is really low."

Tadpole considered this. "Well, if you got in, we should be able to get out."

"Lucky I found a way then," said Lepus.

Tadpole gave his ears a stroke. "Owe you one."

"That makes at least three," chuckled the hare.

★

Henry waited in the darkness, his torch switched off to save the batteries. He decided that, as soon as he heard the door open, he'd make a run for it. At last, as the bolt began to slide back, Henry barged his shoulder into the door as hard as he could. He felt the wood slam into something soft, and then he burst through. A figure lay tumbled on the ground.

Now Henry flicked on his torch and shone it down the tunnel in both directions, searching for the way to the entrance. Before the figure could struggle to its feet, he picked a direction and ran.

A whispered call stopped him dead. "Hen-ree!"

It was Tadpole.

★

Tadpole got to her feet, ignoring her bruised chest, and grabbed Hen-ree's lantern, jabbing at it until the beam died. Then she pulled him flat against the tunnel wall. "Not good, Hen-ree, here. We go," she whispered.

"Go, how?"

Tadpole stared down the passageway. "Lepus, head along this tunnel and check the way is clear. When you get to the main corridor, turn left and keep going until you reach the lifts. Run ahead and warn us if anyone's coming."

With a chirrup, Lepus bounded off. Tadpole raised a finger to her lips, making sure Hen-ree understood, then followed the hare into the gloom.

★

Though Henry knew this was an escape, as he, Tadpole and the hare slunk through the Greybeard home, he couldn't help but marvel at it all. It was like a rabbit warren, smooth passageways branching off in all directions, lit up by the greenish glow of lanterns.

They tiptoed past what looked like a dining hall, full of tables and benches carved from wood, a pottery with shelves of bowls and cups, and a garden with neat rows of vegetables under the blaze of lantern light. Then the hare gave a rapid thump-thump with its foot and Tadpole pushed Henry into a darkened doorway.

A pair of Greybeards ambled past, mumbling to each other, their strides slow and plodding. One of them stopped in the tunnel right in front of them and gave the air a long sniff. Henry held his breath and hardly dared to look. The Greybeard sniffed again, then cocked an ear. Satisfied, he carried on, and the tunnel fell silent again.

Henry gazed round at the cave they found themselves in – strings of what looked like dried insects hung from the ceiling, as well as bunches of lavender. Shelves lined the walls, filled with all manner of jars and jugs. Henry inspected one filled with liquid. Something wriggled underneath the surface, and he recoiled. Then Tadpole tapped him on the shoulder, and they crept out into the next tunnel.

They slipped through the murk, the faint insect glow illuminating a room full of spinning wheels and giant looms, and then into a cavern that seemed to be some sort of arena, with benches looking down on a deep trench filled with mud. They tiptoed by the library, its floor-to-ceiling shelves crammed with books.

On they went, past rows and rows of tidy doors, each with enormous Greybeard-sized mats out the front, and then what Henry assumed was a gymnasium with a large pole, covered in oil, that reached up high. He thought back to his rope climb the other day.

At last, they reached the end of the tunnel that opened

out into a large cavern. At one end stood hollowed-out tree trunks and some darkened shafts that disappeared into the floor. If Henry wasn't mistaken, they were lifts.

Tadpole ducked down, checking that the way was clear, then she grabbed hold of Henry's hand and dragged him towards a tree trunk, shoving him in, and squeezing herself in behind.

Henry's stomach gave a lurch as the trunk dropped down through the dark. He held his breath, his eyes watering. Where was Tadpole taking him? The entrance to the Greybeard home was up near the peak, but she was leading him deeper underground.

The tree trunk reached the end of the shaft with a bump. Tadpole took him by the arm and pulled him behind a fold in the rock. When it seemed as if they were safe, Henry gazed out from behind the stone.

They were in an enormous cave, the biggest Henry had seen so far, lit up by the glow of lanterns high above. Stalactites hung from the ceiling like pillars of white snow, dripping water from their tips into barrels below.

Even at this hour, squads of Greybeards trudged through the gloom, scooping up buckets from the barrels, and feeding them into a giant waterwheel, their movements slow and orderly. A stream of water found its way to a giant funnel at the top of the cave. As the water flowed back down the pipe, other Greybeards stood below, pushing and pulling wooden frames, the water eventually trickling into the huge reservoir. This was some sort of enormous water-filtering machine.

Tadpole followed his gaze. "Clean water," she whispered, then let out a sigh. "But water go small."

Henry looked again at the waterhole; studying the walls, he could see the water was usually much higher. Just like the stream running through the woods.

Tadpole gestured at him to stay put, then came out from behind the rock. She found two empty buckets and crept back, handing Henry one, and showed him how to keep it on his left shoulder, masking his face. Tadpole signalled that she would walk in front. When she was satisfied that he had understood, she again emerged from the shadows and into the cave.

28

Tadpole had so many questions for Hen-ree, but they would have to wait. Right now, they needed to get out of the sett. She took a deep breath and made sure he stayed hidden close behind her, holding his bucket. Tadpole hoped the others were too tired to notice they were there at all – she saw Crewcut on one of the shaking boxes, barely able to keep her eyes open.

As they walked past the waterhole, Tadpole peered in. The water looked to have dropped again. She guessed there was only about five knots left at the bottom, maybe less. Even with her dad's team working flat out all moon long, they just couldn't fill the tank up faster than it emptied. How would the Collective canoes float?

Thinking about her dad brought another wrench to Tadpole's chest. She'd led a human right into the sett, right into Shadowspring. Waterworks and Shipshape would be so ashamed if they found out what she'd done. Tadpole shook the worry from her head and padded for the entrance to the waterway. First, she had to help Hen-ree escape.

★

Tadpole ducked into a channel leading away from the main cave and, once inside, she and Henry dumped their buckets. Further in, the stream split into two. On one side was a wooden dock. The Greybeard kneeled and scooped up a handful of water, and took a long slurp. She gestured at Henry to try some too. He cupped his hands together and slowly brought them to his lips. The water was sweet, like nectar. He took another handful and drained it.

"Good," said Henry.

"Good," Tadpole agreed. She tapped him on the shoulder and pointed down the other branch of the stream. At first she seemed reluctant to step in, but then with a shake of her head, climbed down from the bank. Tadpole waded off into the dark.

Henry stepped into the stream, gasping as the icy water reached into his boots. Doing his best to ignore its frosty grasp, he sloshed along, stumbling over river stones, following the Greybeard. Soon the channel grew smaller and Tadpole walked doubled up. As the cave ceiling got even lower, she got down on her hands and knees, putting the hare on her back, and half pulled, half swam her way along.

Henry studied the crevice. How much smaller did it get? Was this really the only way out on to the mountain? All at once, he found it hard to breathe. What if he got trapped? He remembered the story in the news about a whole football team of boys that got stuck exploring a cave. Was he about to become a headline? Boy Trapped in Cave Ate Worms to Survive. Henry shuddered. He had to trust his friend. He lowered himself into the water, remembering at the last moment to take out the walkie-talkie and his phone, and put them in his backpack. The stream drenched the front of his clothes, and he began to shiver. Feeling along the slippery river rocks, Henry crawled after the big feet of the Greybeard barely visible in the gloom. Together, they inched their way along the stream, the cave roof just high enough for Henry to keep his head above water. He was sure his elbows and knees were sore – if he could even feel them. Henry fought down his panic. All he could do was keep on following.

Then, at last, the darkness began to lighten. Was that daylight up ahead? Henry scrabbled faster, breaking into a smile as the light grew. They squeezed round a small bend, and emerged out on the mountainside. The hare jumped off Tadpole's back and the Greybeard pushed herself up, shaking the water from her fur. Henry got to his feet, shivering uncontrollably as his wet clothes caught the wind. But at least they were out in the open.

A thick cloud hung above their heads, and the first trace of light tinged the sky above the ranges to the east. A whole night had passed! It seemed just minutes since he'd stolen out of Roth Manor. And Henry realised he was exhausted.

★

Tadpole flattened herself against a rock, her fur camouflaged by the stone, and made sure they were alone. No Murmurers round this side of the mountain yet. But Rainstorm would have them out here soon enough. They needed to move on. But first she wanted answers.

"Why come here, Hen-ree?" Tadpole demanded.

The boy held up his hands and gave a long explanation. Tadpole tilted her head.

"Why come Tadpole home?" she asked again.

★

Henry tried again, slower this time. "Men hunt. Bad men."

"Hunt?"

Henry had to show her somehow. He kneeled and found a stick. He pulled out the torch from his bag and turned it on, shielding the light. He began to draw in the dirt: a huge figure running and a smaller figure behind. He tried to show the boars as well he could. Then more stick figures. "Men are coming. See?"

"It's a hunt, Tadpole," Lepus hissed at last. "He's drawing a hunt."

"How do you know what that is?"

The hare shuddered. "I've seen it before. Men chasing my kind, other animals too – birds, deer. They usually bring dogs to track the scent, and their thunderclap sticks, and then they…" Lepus sighed.

Tadpole's eyes widened in alarm. "What?"

But the look in the hare's eyes answered her question.

★

Tadpole muttered something that sounded like a curse. "Bad men come?"

Henry let out a sigh. "Bad men," he agreed.

The Greybeard searched for words. "When men come?" she asked at last.

Henry smoothed over the dirt and drew a picture of the sun rising.

Again Tadpole shook her head and seemed to curse.

★

Tadpole understood now. Why Hen-ree had come. The danger the Greybeards were in. The danger she was in. If this hunt was coming to the mountain, then it was

216

all her fault. Revealing the secret of the sett. Bringing thunderclap sticks down on their heads.

You've really done it this time, she thought. There would be no more shadow plays, no drumming for worms in the wormery, no helping out at the waterhole. She thought of her dad, how much he cared about Shadowspring, how precious the water was to him. All might be lost. Tadpole realized she actually liked working at the waterhole. She'd moaned and groaned so much about sett life. If only things were still so safe, so simple.

Be careful what you wish for, she thought she heard Snowdrift say. But it was just the wind. Grandfather! He'd know what to do. Tadpole reached for the pendant around her neck. *Grandfather! We need help. Humans are coming to hunt us this morning.* But there was only silence.

She tried again. Snowdrift didn't say a word. Why didn't he answer? Did he have nothing more to say? Tadpole rubbed the pendant against her lips. What was it Grandfather had said the last time they spoke?

You must do what your heart tells you is right…

★

From inside his backpack came a squawk that made both Henry and Tadpole jump.

"Henry? Are you there?"

Henry grabbed the walkie-talkie out of his bag. Tadpole

stared at it in horror. "Right here, Murray."

"Where the heck have you been? I've been totally worried sick."

"Been out of signal range – I-I was stuck underground." Henry thought about explaining, but then stopped. "I'll tell you all about it later. I'm here with Tadpole. Has the hunt left?"

"Jarvis and MacNeil are already downstairs with Dad, getting ready. Five minutes? I've told Dad you're not feeling great and want to stay in bed."

"Thanks, Murray. Can you do anything to slow them down?"

"I'll do my best. What are you going to do, Henry? I'm worried."

"I'll think of something."

Henry tried to come up with a plan. From what he could tell, at least two Greybeards had gone back out on to the ranges. There could be more. If the boars picked up Tadpole's scent from the trail and stuck to it, they would soon run into fresh prey. Then things could get ugly. Henry pictured the case in Roth's trophy room.

They needed a way to slow the hunters down.

★

Tadpole looked at Hen-ree, searching his face for clues. What was he thinking? "You said hunters usually bring dogs with them?" she asked Lepus.

"Yes, to track the scent. It's how they find their prey."

Tadpole considered this. "So they like to follow a really strong smell?"

"Especially if it's fresh, they won't give it up," the hare agreed.

★

That's it! thought Henry. What if they laid a different scent trail to distract the razorbacks? It could be enough to lead the hunt away from the mountain. But where? It needed to be as far away from the Greybeard home as possible. Somewhere he and Tadpole could really confuse Roth and the others.

The woods!

"Tadpole, we need to go to the forest," Henry explained, gesturing down the slope.

The Greybeard shrugged her shoulders.

"Go trees!" said Henry. "Men come now!"

★

Hen-ree gestured wildly, trying to explain something. Tadpole followed his arms.

"I think he's pointing towards the woods," said Lepus.

Tadpole was beginning to understand what Hen-ree was on about. "What if we set a different trail, Lepus?

219

Get the hunters lost in the woods?"

"It might work," said Lepus. "Pretty risky, though."

Tadpole tried to think straight. She wondered how they could pull this off. "Lepus, I hate to ask, but I need another favour."

"Sure, Tadpole. Let's go to the woods. I'm right beside you."

Tadpole shook her head. "Could you get back into the sett and give Shipshape and Waterworks a message? Tell them what's going on? Warn the Greybeards to stay inside."

"I'd rather go with you."

Tadpole patted her friend on the back. "I know you would."

Lepus let out a sigh. "All right. What do you want me to say?"

★

Tadpole finished giving instructions to the hare, who took a last look at Henry and then darted off into the gloom back towards the waterway.

With the hare gone, Tadpole gave Henry a nod. "We go trees now."

Henry wasted no more time. He put his pack on his back and set off down the slope, awkward and unsteady on his feet, but he hadn't got far when he felt a tap on his shoulder.

"Hen-ree. Slow."

"Yeah, I know. Sorry."

"Help Hen-ree." Tadpole pointed to her back and bent over, resting her hands on her knees. Did she want to give him a piggyback? Henry pocketed his torch and stood behind her. With a little leap, he was on her back, his hands grasping her shoulders, his feet digging into her sides. Her fur was softer than it looked, but she smelled like a bath-shy goat. Henry wriggled his way up her back and then tapped her on the shoulder. "OK."

Tadpole began to run, her strides lengthening, bounding down through the scrub, her feet meeting the earth with the barest of sounds. When she got to a patch of flat rock, the Greybeard halted for a time, dropping to her haunches before striding downhill once again.

Soon they reached a gorge between two hills, filled with stones cascading down the gully. Tadpole dropped down into the rock falls and sprang from boulder to boulder without pause. Henry clutched her fur, giddy with fright, barely able to hold on. Then they were clear of the rocks and running once again through the coarse grass.

Henry could see they'd come round to the other side of the mountain; the two giant domes lay just further below them. Tadpole carried on running. The sky began to take on brushstrokes of red and orange. Soon it would be daylight.

At last, Tadpole reached the human path and dipped down into a nearby bush to catch her breath. There was a squawk from the walkie-talkie.

"Henry, are you there?" said Murray.

"Receiving."

"We've reached the Ben Bell trail. Heading along the top of the woods."

"Already?"

"I think the razorbacks have picked up a scent, Henry. We're going uphill, I think in the direction of those giant rocks."

Henry peered down the slope. There was no sight nor sound of the hunters yet; they were still far enough away. The cloud continued to drop down. Before long the misty blanket would cover everything. It wouldn't slow down the wild boar, but it would certainly make the going tough for Roth and the others.

"They're coming!" said Henry. "Lay trail!" The Greybeard gave a nod, her eyes fearful.

★

Tadpole took her bearings. Then she began rubbing her back against one boulder, then another. Picking spots at random, she did everything a Greybeard should never do. She rubbed her armpits on the stone; she spat on the ground; she took handfuls of the scrub and rubbed them all over her fur; she left strands of hair hanging in the gorse – all the time going down the mountainside in the opposite direction to the sett.

★

Henry tried to keep up with Tadpole as she crept down the mountain. Dark shapes loomed at them through the mist, towering over their heads. Henry recognized them – the giant stone mounds, rounded and smooth, as tall as a house. He saw that if you wedged yourself in the crevice between the two boulders you might just about manage to climb up. Maybe they should try? But Tadpole carried on down the side of the mounds, rubbing her way along.

★

Tadpole stopped rubbing and froze. She'd heard something caught on the wind. Voices. Muffled by the fog. Hen-ree stood rigid too. Tadpole drew a long breath through her nostrils. She couldn't smell the humans, they were sneaky that way, but wafting down, just faintly at first, was an animal smell. It smelled a little like a pig – she knew some humans kept pigs on their farms to the east. She'd gone out there exploring that one time – trailing the path of the mountain stream to where it fed the human crops. But the smell wafting in on the fog was a different kind of pig – spicy, stronger.

223

Tadpole swallowed. Now she could hear the humans chattering to each other, their feet clomping on the path that lay just uphill. They were making more noise than even a hundred Greybeards peak-running could manage. She dropped down to her haunches and beckoned for Hen-ree to do the same.

Then she saw them. Enormous pigs, thick fur bristling along their backs, creeping out of the mist. The pigs had teeth curling up out of their mouths, dripping with slobber, snouts pressed to the ground, squealing and shrieking. They barrelled along the path, straining on the ropes tied round their necks. Other shapes appeared through the mist – men. Men holding thunderclap sticks. The pigs stopped on the path, sniffing and snorting, uncertain where to go. Tadpole held her breath.

★

"They've got something, Mr Roth! A strong scent. Fresh." Henry guessed it was the groundskeeper talking. "I think it heads off the path, down the slope."

"Are you sure we shouldn't just carry on uphill?"

"The boars are keen to go down, sir."

"Told you those boars were the business, Roth!" said Jarvis. "Look! There's a clump of fur on that bush just here."

"Come on!" Murray's dad replied. "Follow them downhill!"

"Hold on, Dad, my shoelace."

"Not again, Murray! How many times are you going to hold us up? We'll never find the Greybeards at this rate."

Henry followed Tadpole round the edge of the giant domes, his mouth dry. Over his shoulder he thought he could see the outlines of Roth and the others. He stumbled on, his chest heaving. Any moment now, he expected to hear the crack of hunting rifles, bullets zinging over their heads. Feel the sharp tusks of a boar against his legs.

"Should I let the boars off the leash, Mr Roth?" said the groundskeeper.

Please, no, thought Henry.

"I don't think so – we'll lose them in this soup," said Roth.

"This stinking fog!"

"Follow me, Mr Roth. Down the slope towards those boulders. The boars definitely have something."

★

Tadpole grunted to herself. The hunters had abandoned the trail uphill and were heading away from the entrance to the sett. As long as the fog gave them cover, and as long as the spicy pigs tracked her scent, she and Hen-ree could lead them further away. But then what? Hope the men grew tired? It seemed unlikely to Tadpole, but it was all they had. Things were not looking good. She felt her eyes filling, but forced back her tears.

Tadpole clambered down the slope, then turned to sniff the air. The pigs were some way behind them, closing in on the boulders. Then she smelled something else on the wind. Tadpole took a deep breath.

It was Greybeard! Close by. Why hadn't she caught it before? Tadpole raised her head above the brush and inspected the mist. At the top of the stony hillocks behind them she could just about detect two shapes. She sniffed again. Could it be Toothpick and Nutcracker?

A vibration, humming through the air, low and unpleasant, answered her question.

29

Fear hit Henry like a punch to the chest. His heart thumped – adrenaline pulsing through his body. He spun round, certain that an unseen danger was close by. Something even more terrifying than meat-eating boars. A faceless, nameless threat. He had to get away.

Henry grabbed at Tadpole's fur in a panic. "Help!" he whispered. "Something's coming!"

But, instead of running, the Greybeard reached out and covered his ears with her enormous hands.

In an instant, the panic that had gripped his whole body was gone. Henry's heart still raced, but the overpowering terror had vanished. Where had it gone? Was it to do with something he could hear? Henry slipped his own hands under the Greybeard's, sticking his fingers in his ears.

Tadpole gave him a smile and gestured for him to keep them covered.

Tadpole was glad Rainstorm had sent out the Murmuring squads. With Nutcracker and Toothpick Murmuring, the hunters would have to flee. They were safe for now.

But, when the mist parted for a moment, Tadpole let out a gasp. The hunters were still stumbling down the slope, coming their way. They didn't seem bothered by the Murmuring in the slightest. Now they were almost at the mounds.

Then Tadpole saw the strange red coverings on their ears. Like cupped hands. The humans couldn't even hear the Murmuring! Tadpole felt the vibrations rise as the guards got louder and louder. But still the humans plodded on.

"Here!" she heard one of them call. They were closing in on Toothpick and Nutcracker. Then the Murmuring stopped. They'd given up. But the Greybeards were still up at the top and they were trapped.

★

Henry lowered his hands. He let out a long sigh of relief. There was no awful feeling of dread. Whatever had caused him to panic was gone.

"Over here, Jarvis – the boars are at the base of the rocks," Henry heard Roth whisper.

"Watch out."

"I'm right behind you. Do you smell that, MacNeil?"

"Dad, I don't like this," said Murray. "I think we should go back."

"That Greybeard is around here somewhere."

"Somewhere near these boulders."

"Why won't this fog clear?"

"Shhh. Quiet!"

"We need to stop. Can't see a thing."

"Everyone, stop!"

Now Tadpole pointed at her chest, raised two fingers and then pointed towards the top of the giant boulders. Henry understood. A pair of Greybeards was up there. He could hear the boars squealing and pawing the base of the rock.

Henry reached into his pouch for his walkie-talkie and turned off the volume just in case Murray tried to call. Seeing his torch in the jacket pocket reminded him of something. Torch. He thought back to what Mr Dossit had said in class:

The light from the sun hit the man and cast a shadow on the mist ... making it seem like there was a large figure...

★

Tadpole stared with alarm at the lantern in Hen-ree's hand. She hoped he wasn't thinking of turning it on, was he? The bright light would make them stand out like a ray of sunshine. Might as well call the men over and invite them to sit and watch a shadow play.

Tadpole paused. Shadow play…

If they stayed hidden by the bushes and used Hen-ree's bright lantern, could they throw her shadow on the mist? It would be just like shapes on a cloth sheet. Then, if they kept changing position, they could make it appear as if her shadow was in several places at once. It might be enough to confuse the men.

Tadpole began gesturing wildly, first at Hen-ree's lantern and then at herself. *Big shadow*, said her hands. *Now!*

★

Henry gave Tadpole a thumbs up. He found his backup torch and then shifted round so he was pointing downhill. Tadpole stood up and spread her arms out wide. She nodded at him. Henry crouched down on the ground and pressed both the buttons. All at once, an enormous outline, three times the size of the Greybeard, shimmered in the mist, a halo circling its head.

"Look!" a voice shrieked. "There! It's huge!"

"I see it! Away to the right of us!"

"The razorbacks are tracking the wrong scent!"

"I have a shot."

Henry killed the lights and once again the mountainside returned to gloomy fog.

"Did you see the size of it?" gasped Roth.

"The boars still seem certain about these boulders."

"No, we just saw it downhill. Keep your eyes peeled."

Henry ran round to the other side of Tadpole and kneeled. Once again, he turned on both the lights.

"There! Over there!" came the shout. "Down the slope to our left!"

"I see it too!"

"Is it the same one?"

"I think I have it!"

Henry turned out the torches.

"It's gone!"

"Wow, it's quick."

"Everyone just hold on!" Roth shouted. "Murray, where are you?"

"Here, Dad."

"Stay close."

"Nobody move."

Tadpole took Henry's hand and crept downhill, not making a sound. When she came to a large rock, she ducked behind it. Henry adjusted his angle and turned on both torches.

"There it is! What a beast!"

"It's going downhill again."

"Don't let it get away!"

Henry turned the torches off again.

"After me!" cried Roth. "Bring the razorbacks this way."

"Are you sure, sir? We're going round in circles."

"Absolutely! I saw it down there."

Henry and Tadpole slunk away down the hill, the Greybeard making sure she rubbed herself against every rock.

"You were right, sir. The razorbacks have picked up the trail again."

"We've got the Greybeard now, I can feel it!" said Roth.

30

Henry and Tadpole kept moving, using the torches to make shadows, drawing the hunters down towards the forest. The silhouetted shape of the terrain began to reveal itself as the fog thinned. Tadpole sought out a path through the rocks and scrub as Henry kept one hand on the Greybeard's back, grasping a handful of her fur, doing his best to keep up. But he was slow – far too slow. Above them, they could still hear the squealing of the pigs, the thud of footfall as the hunters stumbled down after them.

Then the incline began to level out and they found themselves on a ridge. They dropped to their haunches, panting. Henry heard a voice, too close for comfort.

"The mist is clearing. I could let the boars off the leash – they're still on the scent. I think I could track them."

"Do it!"

Tadpole seemed to understand. She pointed to her back. Without waiting a moment longer, Henry clambered on. Now the Greybeard changed direction and strode out along the ridge. Henry thought he could see the dark woods right below them.

★

Tadpole fled into the trees, her arms swinging, legs flying, bounding from trunk to trunk. She winced as Hen-ree gripped a handful of fur as he struggled to hold on. The spicy pigs were loose now. She could hear their trotters – hear the crunch of the undergrowth. Tadpole ran faster, striding through the trees, her feet barely seeming to meet the earth, her steps long – peak-running like she'd never peak-run before, drawing the hunt further and further away from the sett.

They reached level ground and she came to a stop, straining to listen. The woods around them were silent and still, apart from the gurgle of the stream. Tadpole ducked behind a thick tree trunk. They'd lost the men for now, but they would soon follow. She got Hen-ree to wriggle his way down her back. Staring at the stream, Tadpole saw there was only the faintest of trickles; barely anything was left of the brook. Did that mean Shadowspring was running dry?

Ahead of them, a wooden barrier loomed at the edge of

the woods – beyond that, the trees ended and a meadow began, the green grass catching the early-morning light. Across the grass Tadpole could see a vast human dwelling, hulking and grey, as if carved from stone. She'd looked down on it before from a distance – she recognized the roof – but never this close.

Choosing not to venture near the human dwelling, Tadpole began to stride through the trees again, shadowing the course of the barrier. The pigs would pick up their trail again, but, while the humans tracked her, they weren't anywhere near the other Greybeards. At least they had that.

★

They ran on through the trees just on the edge of the Halbrook grounds. Henry wheezed; he could feel his breath rasping in his chest. He couldn't go on much further. A horrendous squeal cut through the woods some way behind them. The razorbacks were on their trail again and Roth couldn't be that far behind. They would catch up any moment now! Tadpole heard the boars too, and quickened her pace. Over the pounding in his head, Henry heard the jangling of the breakfast bell and he could see the red barn just ahead. If they could only get inside.

Then Henry tripped and pitched forward. He hit the

forest floor, tumbling, spinning, his face pressing into the dirt. Pain surged up his leg. With a groan, he pushed himself up, clutching his ankle.

Tadpole raced back to him. "OK, Hen-ree?"

"We need to keep moving," Henry grunted. He cried out as he got to his feet. Tadpole quickly kneeled in front of him, pointing at her back once again.

★

Tadpole heard the thunder of trotters, an awful screeching. The pigs were gaining on them. As Hen-ree clung on once more, she took off, not sure just how much more her legs had to give. To be safe from the spicy pigs, they would have to leave the forest and cross the barrier – over to the human dwelling. Tadpole came to a stop and, with Hen-ree gripping tight, she stepped up on the first railing and heaved herself over.

Then came a thunder of trotters, a hideous wail. Tadpole spun round as the pigs charged through the trees, grunting and squealing. She caught a glimpse of white foam and sharp tusks before they careered into the barrier. The pigs screeched and pawed at the ground. They stood up on their hind legs, scrabbling at the railings. Now Tadpole imagined she could almost hear the shouts of the hunters in the distance. She and Hen-ree needed somewhere to hide. Hen-ree pointed at the human dwelling ahead of them and Tadpole pushed on, keeping one eye on the snarling pigs as they followed.

★

They ran past Mr Dossit's house and reached the barn, and Henry slid to the ground, taking the weight on one leg. He hopped to the sliding door and gave it a tug, praying that it was somehow unlocked. It stuck at first and then rolled a little.

"In here!"

Tadpole came to his side and heaved, and, with the opening just wide enough, Henry peered in. There was no sign of anyone. He and Tadpole squeezed through the gap and tugged against the handle in a hurry, dragging the door closed. They leaned against the corrugated iron, chests heaving.

What was this place? Henry gulped. A line of towering steel vats took up one half of the vast shed. There were at least a dozen of them, each two storeys high, gleaming and silver. Rows of steel pipes ran from the tanks, spreading out across the barn floor like a maze. Up and down, round and round, through a jumble of barrels, tubs and containers. At the far end of this giant machine stood a polished cylinder, dozens of nozzles running round the outside, and under each stood an empty plastic bottle. What was all this doing on school grounds?

Henry spotted a stack of cardboard boxes in the corner. He hobbled over and reached into one, pulling out a bottle. Pure Origins. He remembered the bottles in the dining hall before the tramp, and at Roth's dinner table. He remembered the rockpool and the hermit crab using plastic for a home.

Tadpole stared in wonder. "What this?"

"Water bottles."

★

Tadpole sniffed at the shiny container in her hands. It smelled of nothing. She tapped at the sides, which were hard despite being almost invisible. Tadpole gave the container a shake and watched the water slosh around inside.

Her gaze rose up to the huge shiny barrels. Was each one full of water too? Tadpole thought about Shadowspring: the waterhole getting lower by the day; the waterways no more than a trickle; the dry stream in the forest. The humans were taking all that water and putting it inside these containers!

Tadpole recoiled as a strange contraption nearby, bright red like fire, began to whirr, accompanied by the sound of rushing liquid. Then the ground rumbled and the dwelling began to shake.

Tadpole moved away from the pile of cardboard boxes, worried they would topple, and pulled Hen-ree close to her. The trembles rattled the whole dwelling, the strange human contraption clattering and jumping about on the ground. Then suddenly the rumbling stopped.

Tadpole went over to the contraption and put her ear close. She could hear a little trickle of water. She traced the red pipe that rose up from the ground to the first giant barrel, and followed it all the way round the dwelling. She tapped the red pipe.

"Take water?"

Hen-ree shrugged. "Yes."

Tadpole scratched her chin, her mind turning. If the humans sucked the water from the ground, was it possible to send it back the other way to Shadowspring?

She pointed at the barrels and then down at the ground. "Go back water, Hen-ree?"

★

Of course! thought Henry. Could they pump it back into the ground?

He went over to study the pump, noticing there was a lever marked with two arrows. Right now, it pointed towards the vats. What if they flipped it the other way?

"Let's find out," he muttered and pulled at the lever, but it wouldn't budge.

Tadpole joined in, wrapping her thick fingers round the metal, and heaved it over with a loud clunk. Henry pressed the big button, and the pump began to whirr and whine, and from the pipe came the sound of rushing liquid.

"I think it's working!" said Henry.

Tadpole hurried over to the nearest vat and scaled the ladder. She inspected the inside through the hole in the top.

She gave Henry a smile. "Water goes small!"

Then a rattle at the sliding door startled them both. Henry spun round, searching for a way out. He ran to the back door and found it locked. There was no choice but to hide. Henry hurried into the shadows behind the steel vats, Tadpole coming down to join him. Then they heard the sliding door rumble open.

"Wetwood?" called a voice, trying its best to sound stern. "I … ah … know you're in there. I saw you run right past my window."

It was Mr Dossit.

Henry peeked out to see the headmaster scanning the plant before marching up to the pump and switching it off. The shed went quiet. Mr Dossit checked behind the cardboard boxes. "I know you're in here somewhere. You shouldn't be, Wetwood. Come out."

Henry signalled to Tadpole to stay where she was and keep quiet, and pushed himself between the vats and out on to the floor of the plant.

"Here, Mr Dossit," he said.

"Aha!" Mr Dossit's moustache wiggled. "What on … ah … earth are you doing in here? You're supposed to be at Roth Manor, aren't you?"

Henry looked at his shoes, silent. Then he found his voice. "I might ask you the same thing, sir," he whispered.

"Excuse me?"

Henry gestured at the plant. "This is a water-bottling plant."

Mr Dossit squirmed. "Yes … ah … yes."

"It's draining the mountain spring, sir."

Mr Dossit gaped. "Well … ah…" he stammered.

"There's hardly any water left. I've seen."

"Now … the thing is … Wetwood…" The colour in

242

the headmaster's face drained away. He clenched and unclenched his fists. "The thing is—"

There was a sudden whirring from the pump.

Henry and Mr Dossit spun round to see Tadpole standing in full view by the red pipe, glowering.

"I … ah … don't … um … ah … Greybeard!" Mr Dossit squealed, staggering back.

"Water go home," Tadpole announced.

Mr Dossit leaned on a stack of cardboard boxes to steady himself. "I … um – it can speak!"

"Her name is Tadpole," said Henry.

Tadpole glared at Mr Dossit and he took another step back. "Is she dangerous?"

Henry shook his head. "Not at all."

"I … ah … will take your word for it."

"The Greybeards are in charge of keeping the mountain spring flowing, sir. They're peaceful."

"What do you … mean?" asked Mr Dossit.

"That's their job. Looking after the water below the mountain. Filtering it, keeping it clean," said Henry. "The whole valley depends on them."

"Water clean," said Tadpole.

"They do all the work, only for it to be stolen right out of the ground," said Henry.

Mr Dossit gulped. "It was never my idea… I … I…" He hung his head. "I should never have agreed."

Through the thin corrugated iron came shouting. "They've tracked it into the plant," came a voice.

Then Roth called out. "Put the razorbacks back on the leash and lead them through the gate."

"This Greybeard better be there, Roth."

"Is that Jarvis and MacNeil?" gasped Mr Dossit, staring in horror at the door.

Henry heard Murray cry out, "Dad, you can't go into the school grounds with guns."

"Stay behind us, Murray!"

"They're hunting us, Mr Dossit," said Henry. "There's no time to explain. We need to hide Tadpole."

Mr Dossit searched the plant. His eyes fell on the steel containers. "Into one of the vats," he whispered. "The water will mask her scent. Turn the pump off again and get her to climb in."

★

Tadpole stared at the inside of the giant barrel, almost filled to the top with water. They wanted her to get into *that*?

Hen-ree pointed inside again. He seemed sure.

Tadpole could hear the voices of the hunters outside clearly now. They were getting closer. She heaved herself up on to the top of the barrel and lowered herself through the gap. She hung on to the edges of the hole.

"Bye, Hen-ree," she whispered.

"Out soon," he replied.

Then Tadpole let go of the edges and dropped down, cold water soaking her fur. Hen-ree closed the lid on the barrel and suddenly it was pitch dark. Tadpole couldn't feel the bottom of the barrel because the water was too deep. Could she stay afloat? With the frosty water weighing her down, and the darkness that seemed to close in, Tadpole wished she was back in the den with her mum and dad. Would things ever be like they were before?

A loud scrabbling and banging on the corrugated iron and an awful squealing announced the hunt was at the barn door. Henry scurried down the ladder and ducked into the shadows as the sliding door rattled open. The boars scrabbled over the concrete floor, just about held back by the groundskeeper, followed by Roth and the others. Murray looked miserable.

"Dossit!" hissed Roth when he saw the headmaster.

"What are you doing in the plant?" demanded MacNeil.

"I … ah…" Mr Dossit began.

The boars let out a loud squeal, dragging the groundskeeper towards the vats. "Something's here – the razorbacks seem certain!" he cried.

Jarvis pointed. "Over there, behind those containers."

"The beast!" said MacNeil.

"There's definitely a scent."

Jarvis gripped his rifle. "Get ready!"

"Don't shoot!" Henry shouted. "It's just me back here. Don't shoot!"

While the groundskeeper hauled the boars back outside, Roth took off his earmuffs and paced the plant, glaring at Henry and Mr Dossit, more like an irritated ostrich than ever before. Murray shrank back.

"What on earth is going on, Dossit?" Roth growled. He stopped and pointed at Henry. "And you – you're meant to be sick in bed!"

"A little prank, Mr Roth," said Henry.

"It won't spoil our Greybeard hunt, if that was your idea," said Roth.

"But there is no Greybeard to hunt," said Henry.

"We saw it in the trees," Jarvis snarled.

Henry shook his head. "You saw a Brocken spectre."

"A what?" said MacNeil.

Henry slipped his backpack off and took out the two torches. "You see, I used these to throw a beam, then I stood in front of it and made outlines in the fog – a monster shadow. Then I changed direction and did it again. Did the figure seem to move around a lot?"

"It did!" said MacNeil. "Uphill, downhill, left, right."

"There, you see?"

"Brocken spectre … an … ah … illusion of shadow and mist," said Mr Dossit.

Unconvinced, Jarvis took out his phone and spoke into it. "Brocken spectre."

The phone bleeped, then began to recite. "Brocken spectre. From the German *Brockengespenst*. An enlarged shadow cast upon mist or fog opposite the source of light. Often the shadow appears to be of a giant, many ti—" Jarvis switched off his phone.

"See? And then I ran for the school grounds and hid in here," said Henry.

Now Murray, who'd had his eyes glued to the ground the whole time, spoke up. "We thought the whole thing up last night."

"I can't believe it, Murray!" Roth shook his head. He took the torches from Henry and inspected them. "I saw the photo on your phone."

"More shadows. I did try to say, Mr Roth," said Henry.

"It all makes perfect sense to me. I certainly don't see a hair in here." MacNeil gestured at the plant. "The boars were tracking that boy's scent. There's a pong about him all right. You rascals have had us chasing up and down after nothing."

"And this is your idea of a big joke," Jarvis growled at Murray. "Completely ruining our sport on purpose. You need to keep an eye on that son of yours, Roth."

Roth's face turned a deep shade of red. "I beg your pardon?"

"Little blighter," said MacNeil.

"The boy needs disciplining," added Jarvis.

"Agreed," said MacNeil.

"I'd watch what you say about Murray." Roth clenched his fists. "If you know what's good for you."

Murray looked up at his father. Henry could see his friend almost allowing himself a smile.

Mr Dossit went over to the sliding door and heaved it open. "And I think it's time for you two to leave." He gestured at the giant vats. "Then you can tell your people to take ... all this away."

"Oh, be quiet, Dossit," said MacNeil.

"I've been quiet for ... ah ... too long!"

"Don't forget how you're paying for your new English department," said Jarvis. He turned to Roth. "Or how you're saving your house."

"I do, to my great shame," said Mr Dossit. "But we're draining ... um ... the ground dry."

"Pah," said MacNeil. "There's plenty of water to go around."

"It stops now," said Dossit. "If you don't get off the grounds at once, I will call the police, and you can explain why you brought guns and savage boars on to school property. And we can *all* explain how we're taking water without a permit." Henry had never seen Mr Dossit look so furious, or his moustache waggle so much.

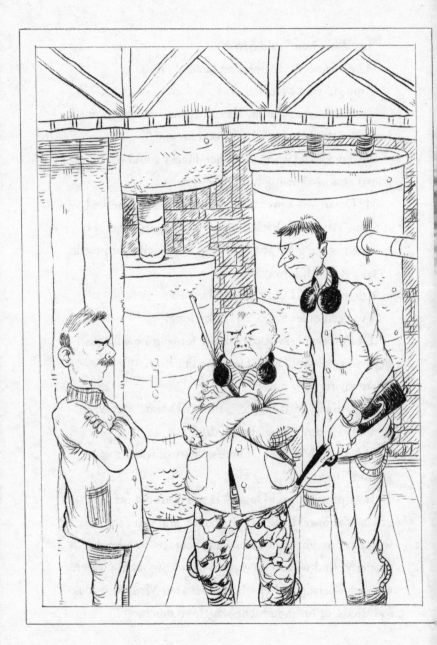

"You wouldn't," said MacNeil.

"I would."

There was silence. Jarvis and MacNeil glanced at each other.

"Come on, MacNeil," said Jarvis at last.

"We'll see you ruined for this, Roth!" said MacNeil as they sloped out of the shed.

Once they had left, Roth slumped on to the cardboard boxes. "Well, that's me done for, Dossit."

Murray went over and sat beside him. "It'll be all right, Dad."

"There's no way to save the house now," sighed Roth.

"Then perhaps we don't have to go on pretending like we're the lords of the manor any more," said Murray. "I'm not like those other Roths and I don't think you are either."

Henry smiled. He could hardly believe this was his room-mate speaking.

Roth looked up at his son, dumbfounded. "I see."

All at once a loud banging came from inside the container.

★

Tadpole couldn't take any more of it. By putting herself at full stretch, she'd managed to press against both sides of the water container, helping her to stay afloat, but the icy water and the total darkness were too much. She'd heard angry voices through the sides of the tank.

I'll just have to give up, thought Tadpole. *Hope for the best.* She reached out of the water and gave the side of the tank another thumping.

★

"There it is again. What is it?" asked Roth, peering at the far end of the plant.

"Probably just the pipes," said Henry.

"No, it was coming from over there," said Roth.

Henry glanced at Dossit.

"Well … ah … um…" was all the headmaster could manage.

A bang came from inside the vat. Then another.

"What's inside that container?" demanded Roth.

BANG!

Henry couldn't leave his friend trapped in the dark any longer. He hurried over to the tank and scaled the ladder. At the top, he turned the handle, and lifted the lid.

Everyone watched in awe as the Greybeard hauled herself out of the tank, water pouring from her fur and cascading over the side of the container. She looked cold and miserable.

"Sorry, Tadpole," said Henry.

"No way!" said Murray.

"Greybeard!" Roth spluttered. "I knew it!"

Henry climbed down the ladder, Tadpole following, dripping water all over him. They came from behind the tanks.

"Meet Tadpole," said Henry.

★

There were four humans now. Hen-ree and another youngling, the tall one with a poor excuse for a moustache and a reedy one that reminded her of a heron. Her secret was well and truly out.

The humans were arguing among themselves. Or rather Hen-ree and the moustache were doing lots of gesturing and talking while stork stood and took it all in – his fearful eyes fixed on her the whole time. Tadpole could only manage to catch a few of the words.

Water. Wrong. Back.

Then, when it looked like Hen-ree and the moustache had finished talking, the heron man shuffled over to the contraption and pressed the big button. The contraption began to whine again and Tadpole heard the rush of water. He was putting it back.

★

At last, the water pump in the plant began to splutter and cough. Henry smiled. They'd done it.

"I think that's the last of it," Mr Dossit called out, punching the button.

Tadpole gave a satisfied chortle.

Henry slumped to the ground, joining Murray who was leaning back against the wall. Around them, every cardboard box lay open, the contents of each bottle poured back into one of the vats and pumped back into the ground.

"That's an awful … lot of plastic," sighed Mr Dossit. "Seeing it all piled up like that makes you realize. Such waste."

"Imagine how many more plastic bottles like this there are in the world," said Henry.

"I shudder to think," said Mr Dossit and they all stared in silence.

"So now what happens?" asked Murray at last.

"Tadpole needs to get home. She's already in serious trouble – trust me."

"Ah… Then I think that we must make sure her kind are left in peace," said Mr Dossit. "Tadpole and the Greybeards have to stay secret. Especially from Jarvis and MacNeil."

"If it gets out, we won't be able to stop people coming," said Henry. "We all have to swear."

Mr Dossit held out his hand. "We … ah … make a solemn pledge."

One by one, Henry and the others shook his hand.

Tadpole watched, puzzled, then did the same.

Henry held his finger up to his lips and pointed to the others. "No speak." He could see she understood.

Tadpole prodded Roth in the chest with a thick finger. "No find Tadpole. No hunt."

"No hunt," said Roth.

Now Mr Dossit went over and stuck his head through the gap in the sliding door. "Luckily the fog has rolled in again. If the Greybeard is … quick, she could … ah … slip down the side of the barn and back into the trees without anyone seeing."

Tadpole turned to Henry. "Tadpole go home."

"Are you going to be OK?" Henry asked.

Tadpole shook her head. "Tadpole bad."

"I wish I could help."

"No help." Tadpole sighed.

"Take care of yourself." Henry was about to shake her hand, then remembered. Instead, he tapped his chest and then his head.

Tadpole gave him a smile and returned the salute. Then, with a final look at the inside of the plant, she slipped through the gap and out into the mist.

★

Tadpole had never wanted to feel Mum and Dad's hugs so badly, to climb into her nest and hide. But what sort of welcome could she expect? She'd brought them all so close to danger. Tadpole took her time to reach the peak. She found a place between two boulders to catch her breath. Maybe none of it had happened at all? She might find herself back in her den and realize it was just in her head like her chats with Grandfather.

She got to her feet to make the final few strides to the sett entrance. Then two shapes loomed at her through the mist. Tadpole took a deep breath. She recognized those smells. It was Toothpick and Nutcracker.

The guards were at her side in a flash.

"Sweet whiskers," said Nutcracker.

"We were so worried. When those men…" Toothpick wrapped Tadpole in her arms.

Tadpole flinched. Was Toothpick giving her a hug? "I'm fine," she said, surprised.

"Thank goodness," said Nutcracker.

"You rescued us," said Toothpick.

"You and that human boy," said Nutcracker. "We saw."

Tadpole gave a weak smile. "I guess we did."

"I'm afraid Rainstorm and the elders want to speak to you," said Nutcracker. "You've caused quite the stir."

"I know." Tadpole's throat felt tight.

Toothpick took her by the arm. "Now you'd better come with us. They're waiting."

The guards led Tadpole down the deep crevice and

Nutcracker pounded the secret knock on the rock door. Tadpole winced with each blow of his fist. The door would open soon, and there was no escaping now. What lay on the other side?

As the doorway slowly lifted, Tadpole caught the first glimpse of dozens of hairy feet.

"She's here," she heard someone say.

"About time," said another.

Tadpole braced herself for the anger and the scolding. Cold silence greeted Tadpole as the guards marched her in. She heard the boulder drop down behind her with a thud. Tadpole kept her gaze on the ground, her eyes filling with tears, her legs trembling. Then gingerly she raised her head to meet the crowd, searching for Shipshape and Waterworks.

"Three cheers for Tadpole!" a shout filled the cave.

"Hurrah!" came the reply. "Hurrah! Hurrah!"

Tadpole staggered back. All she could see were smiles. What was this?

"Good on you, Tadpole!"

"Keeping the humans from the sett!"

"Well done, Tadpole!" Several Greybeards came to give her a pat on the back.

Tadpole spotted her parents in the crowd, Lepus in her dad's arms. They pushed their way through and Shipshape gathered Tadpole in a squeeze.

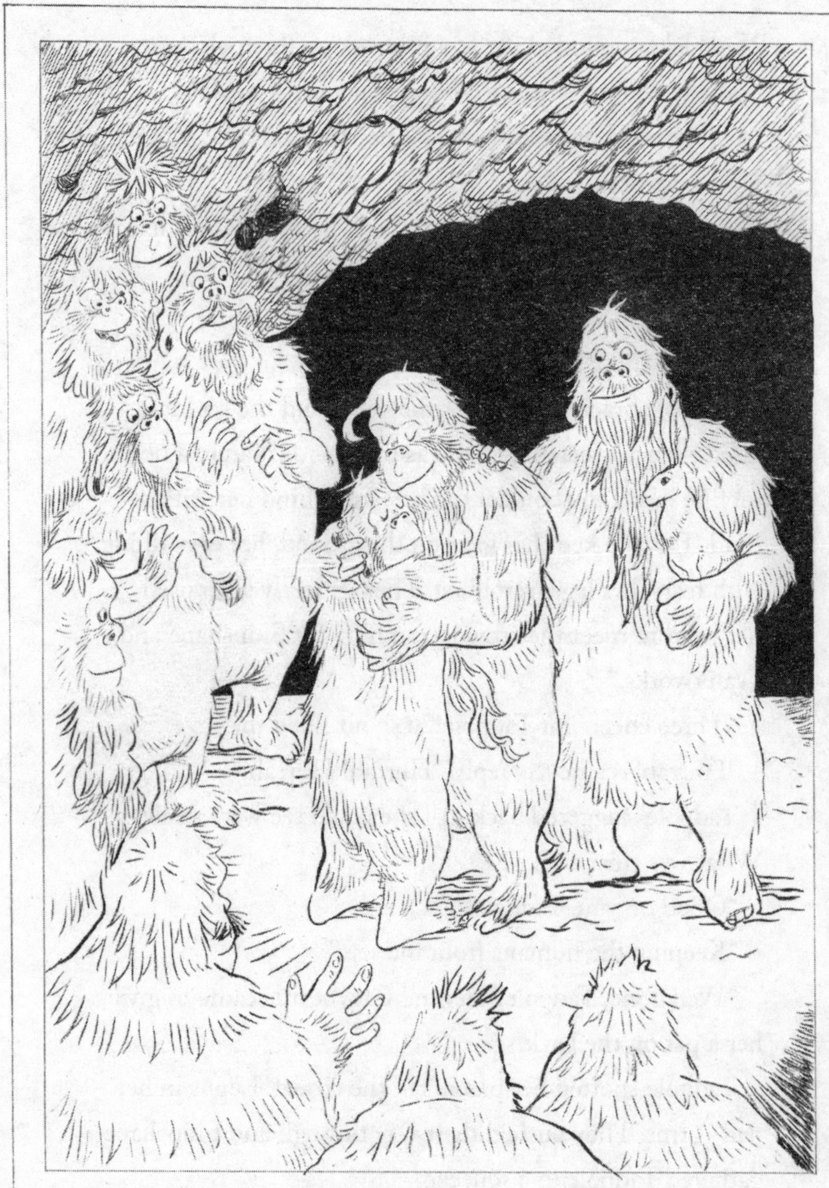

"Thank goodness you're back! We've been worried out of our shaggy heads," she said.

"Are you all right?" asked Waterworks, looking her up and down. His eyes filled with tears.

"When we got Lepus's message, we were so scared," said Shipshape. "But we listened to your warning."

"I made sure the rest stayed inside just like you said." Lepus gave his friend a smile. "I told them they could trust you to fix things, Tadpole."

"Thanks, Lepus."

"And you did it, Tadpole. You saved the sett," said Shipshape.

Waterworks wiped his tears away and grinned. "Somehow Shadowspring is at twelve knots and climbing!"

"You're not cross?"

"Oh, we're cross," admitted Shipshape.

"But when things were tough you did what was right, Tadpole," said her dad.

Tadpole gave them both another long hug, until Lepus kicked out with his legs and gasped, "Mercy!"

Then Hindsight banged her staff on the floor and broke up the gathering. "Let's get back to work, Greybeards, if you please! You can talk to Tadpole later."

As the Greybeards dispersed down the tunnel, Rainstorm came over to join them. "I'm glad to see that you are safe, youngling."

"Thank you, O Rainstorm," said Tadpole, remembering her manners. She bowed. "*The best-laid plans of mice and Greybeards often go awry.*"

Rainstorm nodded. "And *actions speak louder than words*, Tadpole. I hear you have been very brave. Before we discuss things further, I must ask, is the sett still in any danger?"

"No. I don't think so. The humans promised to leave us well alone. They gave me their word." Tadpole suddenly felt very weary. It had been a long night.

"Assuming we can trust what they say," muttered Rainstorm. "Now about—"

"Could it not perhaps wait, Rainstorm?" suggested Shipshape. "The poor youngling can barely keep her eyes open." She put a protective arm round Tadpole's shoulder. Tadpole leaned into her.

Rainstorm nodded. "Fair enough. But there are still many questions. We shall meet in the morning, and *don't count your grouse until they are hatched.*"

Hi,

Karman told us over breakfast that the manuscript is gone. He showed us a pile of burnt ashes in the stove and says he burned it in the middle of the night to heat the kettle to make tea.

Dad started banging his head on the kitchen table.

Karman told him not to be so dramatic and that in a few years he'll deliver us a proper masterpiece, and not a pile of drivel that didn't deserve to be read.

We're leaving Hungary. As soon as we get back home, we'll come and get you from school. I'll let you know our travel plans when we've made them.

Love Mum

33

When Tadpole woke up in her darkened den, for a moment she thought she was still in the awful water barrel of the humans. But the soft glow of the fireflies and the even softer moss blanket pulled up round her chin told her otherwise. Tadpole let out a long breath. She was safe in her own nest. Low voices came from the living den.

Tadpole struggled to get up, her legs sore. She could barely stand upright. Every hair on her body felt limp. She splashed water on her face and stumbled into the living den.

The silverback and the Guardian were waiting with her mum and dad, their hands wrapped round mugs of hot gorse juice.

"Morning, my love," said Waterworks. "Sleep well?"

"I'll get you some nibbles," said her mum.

Tadpole slumped down. The others waited patiently

until she'd eaten and drunk.

"Now I think you need to tell us everything, Tadpole."
Rainstorm pointed at Hen-ree's book sitting on the low
table in front of them. "Starting with that. How did that
human boy get a map to the sett?"

Tadpole took a deep breath. "I first met the human boy
by accident when I was getting the *specktakulls* – to help
Mum to see."

"You *knew* she was meeting the human, Shipshape?"
said Rainstorm.

"No, of course not," said Shipshape. "This is the first
I'm hearing of it."

"Where did you get those *specktakulls* from?" asked
Waterworks.

"From a human hut. Snowdrift knew a human. Called
Hazel. She was Grandfather's friend." Tadpole's words
came out in a garble, and then she burst into tears.

"Snowdrift!" said Rainstorm. "Human hut?"

"You're not making any sense, my love. Now calm down
and try again," said Shipshape.

Tadpole took a deep breath. "The story really begins
with him. Cycles ago, Snowdrift went out peak-
running…"

Tadpole told them everything. All that she knew about
Snowdrift and Hazel meeting by accident. How Snowdrift
considered humans kin – that they were once one of

Earth Mother's children – it said so in the slabs. Tadpole explained how Grandfather had learned a little human tongue and taught her some words too. How the map on the pendant showed how to find Hazel's secret hut.

"Hen-ree must have copied out the map when I left it behind at the hut by accident." She gestured at the book on the bench.

"I can't believe Dad never told me any of this." Waterworks stared at the symbols on the clay. "You think you know your parents…" His eyes began to fill.

Tadpole spoke about finding the *specktakulls*. She described Hen-ree tumbling into the hollow. The second meeting. Then later how she rescued him and helped him escape from the sett.

"Sweet whiskers," said Rainstorm.

"Men were coming to track us down. Hen-ree took a big risk to come and warn us," said Tadpole. "Grandfather was right: not all humans are bad."

Then Tadpole told them about the showdown on the hillside, the hunters with their guns and spicy pigs. How she and Hen-ree fooled them with a shadow play in the mist. How they drew the humans away from the sett and towards the giant human dwelling.

"You used your shadow plays?" gasped Shipshape.

Finally Tadpole told them about the scene in the dwelling and the strange contraptions inside that sucked the water from the mountain.

Waterworks let out a whistle. "So that explains it."

"And you were just saying humans aren't all bad," said Hindsight.

"But they've stopped now. They also helped me put the water back," Tadpole argued.

"Up to seventeen knots this morning," agreed Waterworks.

Rainstorm stayed silent, thinking, his fingers running along the length of his sash.

Tadpole waited. Had she done enough to unravel all the bad things she'd done?

"Tadpole, *she of unripe character*, where do we even start with all your wrongdoings?" Rainstorm began at last. "Visiting a human dwelling. Meeting a human. Speaking with this human. Allowing the whereabouts of the sett to fall into human hands. Enabling a human to come to our very door."

"The slabs are clear in these matters. Each of the charges on their own carries the penalty of banishment," said Hindsight.

Tadpole swallowed.

"But, while your mistakes were indeed grave, in each case your actions were done out of a sense of duty," said Rainstorm. "I, for one, have misjudged you, Tadpole."

"And I," said Hindsight.

The silverback continued. "It is said that *when the going gets hairy, the hairy get going.* Your brave deeds saved two guards from certain danger and protected the sett from the hunt. You were also able to return the water the humans stole." Rainstorm paused. "I therefore rule that we overlook all charges."

Tadpole broke into a grin.

The silverback got to his feet. "Now there is much to be done! We expect the Gathering very soon!"

★

The next week, when his parents had got back from their trip, Henry led them and headmaster Dossit through the trees and along the bank of the gushing stream, Murray by his side, their breath just starting to show in the cold autumn morning. It wasn't just the seasons that were changing: quite a lot else had happened since (what Henry was calling) 'the showdown in the shed'.

According to Murray, things had deteriorated further with his dad and Jarvis and MacNeil. The plant was being dismantled and taken away. Now that he was bankrupt, his dad had to put Roth Manor up for sale.

"It's the only way," said Murray.

"Are you going to miss it?" asked Henry.

"Nah. We never needed such a big place anyway," said Murray. "Apparently, the council wants to buy it and turn it into a hospital. Much better. And, when the place sells, Dad is talking about us taking some time off to go and visit Mum in Spain. They're going to take me to the Picasso Museum too."

"What's happening to those boars?"

"A wildlife park wants to take them. Good luck with that!"

★

After getting back from Hungary, Henry's mum and dad came straight up to collect him. They were a little surprised when he told them that he'd chosen to stay on until the end of the year.

"Look, it's lovely walking through the woods with you boys, but what's the big secret?" Henry's dad asked as he pushed through the undergrowth along the banks of the gushing brook.

"I … ah … must confess, I'm as much in the dark as … you," said Mr Dossit.

"We're almost there," said Henry as the boulders in the middle of the woods came into view.

"It's worth it, Mr and Mrs Wetwood," Murray added.

Henry stopped at the gap in the stones. "In there and up the stairs." He pointed at the crevice. "Then you'll see."

★

The notebooks lay on the table, just where Henry had left them. Now he and Murray sat up in the bunk, legs dangling, while Henry's parents read the first notebook together. The boys sat in silence for a while, listening to the turning of the pages. Mr Dossit was out investigating the hollow.

"Listen to this, boys," said Henry's dad, breaking the silence. He read a passage aloud:

"*The castle faced the sea. Its cold stone walls had stood for two hundred years and would probably stand for two hundred more. Rows of cannons bristled along the castle battlements facing the channel. A lookout was there on the walls, though he only gave the sea a casual glance. Below, a deep moat ran round the castle, dark and fetid. Birds picked through the mud and filth. Tiny slit windows crossed with iron bars looked out on the foul moat: the dungeons.*

"*A cart rumbled across the drawbridge, the sound scattering the seagulls below. It stopped in the gloom of the gatehouse underneath enormous arches. Sebastian shivered in the shadows, his feeling of despair deepening.*"

"This is good," said Mr Wetwood. "You were right, Henry."

Henry grinned. "So you think it might be worth publishing?"

"Of course, we'll need to read the whole thing." His mum looked up from the table. "But I really like what I see so far."

Dad gave a quiet laugh. "Just think, we went all the way to Hungary to find our next book and instead it's been sitting in a bothy in the woods called Budge."

"Life can be funny at times." Mrs Wetwood gathered all the notebooks into a tidy pile and put them in her bag.

Leaving everything as it was, Henry closed the door to Budge behind them.

Out in the hollow, Mr Dossit sat on a rock, contemplating Hazel's grave.

"I'm still ... quite stunned," he murmured. "To think this is where Hazel Halbrook ended up."

"Surprising, isn't it, sir?" agreed Henry.

"She was quite a formidable headmistress, passionate about learning and the mountains, but ... a very private person at the same time."

"I guess that explains a secret hut in the woods," said Henry. "She wanted to stay close."

"And ... now we know ... ah ... where."

"Did she have any family? They might like to know about this place." Henry's mum nodded at the grave. "Come and pay their respects."

"None that I'm aware of. She was the last of her line," said Mr Dossit. He glanced round the hollow. "What a charming spot ... though. I'm glad it's been left untouched all these years."

"We won't tell anyone," said Henry, and Murray agreed.

Back in the grounds of Halbrook, they found Mrs Nettles watching the workers down at the shed loading a steel vat on to the back of a lorry.

"Ah … looks like we're just in time to see the plant being removed," said Mr Dossit. "Now we … ah … just have to find a way to pay for our new English department."

Henry's mum patted her bag. "If things go well with Hazel Halbrook's novel, perhaps we can help you there."

"Now wouldn't that be something?" said Mr Dossit.

"Hazel Halbrook?" asked Mrs Nettles.

"I'll explain later, Mrs Nettles," said the headmaster. "Now can I … offer everyone a cup of tea?"

Henry's dad shook his head. "We'd better head off if we want to catch the train back to London. I've already called a cab."

"We'll be back at the end of the year," said his mum.

"I'm off too, Mr and Mrs Wetwood. Krish and Bony are waiting to play Vault and Serpent," said Murray, climbing the steps. "Turns out it's an amazing game. Even Fraser and Fletch want to give it a go. Didn't see that coming."

When the taxi pulled up, Henry went to see his parents off. Before they got in, he gave them both a kiss and a massive hug – and he didn't care who was watching.

34

It was several moons before the bat messenger swooped in and the Greybeards learned that the Collective were practically on their doorstep. Once Flittermouse latched on to Lukewarm's arm, the message soon spread across the sett: the Mande Barung would be there shortly, the other members of the Collective probably not that far behind.

"They're here!" said Tadpole when word reached her at the top of the ladder. On instructions from Hindsight, Tadpole finished the last corner of the tunnel wall, and started collecting up her things.

"Everything must be put away. I want these tunnels clear," the Guardian ordered. "Then down to Shadowspring."

Tadpole ran to join the others. As she padded down the tunnel, she saw Greybeards everywhere adding final touches: rows of centipede tarts lined the kitchen bench ready for dinner, moss pillows were fat and plump in the nests and, in the pottery, she saw the last of the plates were out of the kiln and cooling down.

Shadowspring was buzzing. The welcoming choir gathered at the entrance to the water tunnel, Upstage getting them to their places. Tadpole saw Rainstorm, his hair brushed back, the Stinking Sash sitting on his chest, leading the Council of Elders towards the landing dock. Tadpole tried to catch Shipshape's eye at the back of the procession, but she was soon lost in all the commotion. Tadpole was jostled into place beside Tagalong.

"This is so exciting," said Tagalong. "I heard it's the Mande Barung coming first. They brought a flock of bats with them."

From the row behind, Slapstick gave a snort. "Flock of bats! It's one bat." He pointed to the flying fox swooping and soaring above the crowd.

From deep in the water channel came the bellowing of a horn. All at once, the hubbub in Shadowspring dropped and the workers turned to face the tunnel. Now there was just the soft trickling of water and the odd Greybeard stomach growling.

"This is it. Ready to go from the top. And don't you dare try and come in early again and throw us all off, Scapegoat," whispered Upstage. "On my signal."

Tadpole swallowed and took a deep breath. Upstage

raised her arm and, as a cheer broke out from the landing dock, she brought it down.

You know what they say…
Hold the stone as one and it won't feel heavy,
A good buttock deserves a comfortable seat…

Once the ambassadors of the Mande Barung landed at the Greybeard dock (Tadpole was amazed at Leeke the elder, her eyes pale blue like summer sky), the other setts began to arrive in a steady procession. The choir belted the greeting song to each arriving sett until their voices could take no more.

The elders shepherded each yeti into the lifts and up to their lodgings, porter Greybeards followed with their belongings and, with the final canoe tied up at the dock, the welcoming committee squeezed into the lifts, and joined them. The cavern soon fell quiet once more, apart from Waterworks and his team, who had plenty to do now the water barrels were once again filling up apace.

When Tadpole joined the others in the sett, she could see their guests were too excited to worry about resting weary limbs, and soon they climbed out of the nests in their lodgings and gathered in the meeting hall. Over cups of hot heather mead, the yeti began to introduce each other, saluting and bowing. Proverbs and sayings filled the air, and the stench wafting over the cavern was most agreeable. The Bigfoot and the Sasquatch took it upon themselves to begin a spell of line dancing.

It struck Tadpole that none of the ambassadors had ever met yeti from another sett before – except for the two Mountain Yeti, the famous Plumm and Tick, just a few cycles older than her, who greeted the Makimaki and Mande Barung like long-lost kin. A tiny Orang Pendek with the most impressive braid of long hair leaped into Tick's arms.

Before long, curiosity took over and the guests drifted out of the meeting hall to poke their noses round the sett. Tadpole followed them out. Soon the yeti flung wet rags in the flonking pit and slid to the ground with a thud off the greasy pole. The elder of the ambassadors inspected the books in the library and settled into soft chairs.

The meetings would start soon. There was so much to discuss: the plight of bees; the coral reefs; shrinking ice; frogs and toads; the growing heat. And, of course, what to do about the mess the humans were making of everything.

Tadpole met Shipshape outside the slop-snorkelling room. Roars came from the spectators, including Rainstorm and Hindsight who were both up on their feet, cheering. From what Tadpole could tell, one of the Mande Barung appeared to be winning.

"It seems like just yestermoon that you and your friends

were the ones causing a ruckus in here," said Shipshape. "And, thanks to these, I can actually see what's going on." She tapped the *specktakulls* perched on her nose.

"I'm glad Lukewarm decided to give them back to you – human contraptions or not."

"I guess I've had trouble seeing a lot of things, Tadpole." Shipshape took her hand. "That your shadow plays were so important to you. That you didn't want to be a silverback. That you wanted a different path than the life your dad and I had all planned out for you."

"That's OK, Mum." Tadpole blushed.

Shipshape gave her an eyelash kiss. "Thanks, Tadpole."

"Actually, after all the kerfuffle, it turns out I quite like our life down here in the sett. Maybe I could have been a silverback."

Shipshape glanced round the room at the happy yeti. "It's not bad, is it?"

Tadpole gestured at Rainstorm on the viewing stand. "You don't miss the sash, Mum?"

"A little," she admitted. "But there are more important things in life." She gave Tadpole's hand a squeeze. "Besides, I think Rainstorm will turn out to be a good leader. He's stopped the Murmuring, by the way."

"Really?"

"He reckons it did more harm than good. There's been enough chasing," said Shipshape. "Yes, things are back to where they ought to be. And, best of all, plenty of fresh water for the Greybeards, the trees and even the humans."

Tadpole felt a hand on her shoulder. It was Waterworks. "What did I miss?"

"The Mande Barung are fantastic slop-snorkellers," said Tadpole.

"I hear their sett is up in the trees. I'd love to see that," said Shipshape.

"Well, you know, the Council still haven't decided which of us Greybeards will get to travel when the Gathering is over," said Waterworks. "I was wondering if we should put our hands up."

"Really?"

"Of course, we'd need to take someone along who knows how to sneak down waterways, and how to speak to a human if we happened to run into one," said Shipshape.

Tadpole laughed.

"Just keep it in mind," said Waterworks. "I'll save you a spot in the canoe."

"Two," said Tadpole. "I'm sure Lepus would like to come."

"Two," agreed Shipshape.

EPILOGUE

While all the festivities were in full swing, Tadpole led Tick and Plumm of the Mountain Yeti through the entrance cave towards the surface. Tadpole squeezed through the narrow crevice and, when she was sure the hillside was clear, she beckoned to the others to follow. Tadpole pointed down the mountain at the woods in the distance.

"So the human dwelling you were telling us about is hidden in that forest down there?" asked Tick.

"I wish I could take you to see Hazel's place. Show you where the adventure began." Tadpole tilted her head back and sniffed, catching nothing but the moisture on the wind. "But with the extra security I had to beg the guards just to let us peek our heads out for a moment – they owed me one."

"I still can't believe you live so close to humans,"

whispered Plumm. "Yeti Mountain is strides and strides away from the nearest human dwelling. We hardly ever see them."

"You get used to it," said Tadpole. She added, "Some of us more than others."

Tick chuckled. "Glad to know I'm not the only one in the Collective who gets into trouble with people. Sounds like my friend Ell-a would get on with your friend..."

"Hen-ree."

"I wonder whether this will change anything," said Plumm. "Will the Collective decide we yeti can work with humans?"

"My grandfather, Snowdrift, always said that we are like fingers on the same hand," said Tadpole. "We exist for one another – stronger together than apart."

Thinking about him, Tadpole felt for her pendant. She already knew Snowdrift wouldn't pop up and talk. The clay didn't work like that any more. But he would always be her grandfather – she would remember what he taught her, the time they spent together, and that would never change.

And, wherever Snowdrift and Hazel happened to be right at this moment, perhaps some hut in another hollow somewhere, Tadpole wanted them to know that, all in all, things had turned out well in the end.

"Fancy some slop-snorkelling?" she asked the others, turning to go back. "I do this crazy dive. You should see it…"

ACKNOWLEDGEMENTS

I owe so many thanks: for the never-ending flow of support and creativity from my wife Jenny; for my editor Ruth Bennett's guiding hand and astute counsel (not to mention the inspired title); Katy's illustrations, which make the story soar; Jane Tait's attention to detail in the copyedit; Sophie Bransby's flair for design; and Leilah Skelton, Lauren Ace, Ella Whiddett and the team at Stripes for bringing Shadowspring out into the world. This is our book. Thank you.

Among other yeti folklore, the story draws inspiration from Scottish tales of Am Fear Liath Mòr, the Big Grey Man of Ben Macdhui, as well as wonderful sayings and proverbs from countries across the world.

When I began writing Shadowspring, I wanted to create a character based on my father, David. Snowdrift and David have much in common: they are ready with good advice, handy tiddlywinkers and share a passion for pottery. (They also both have snow-white beards!) More importantly, they are kind and caring. Sadly before he got a chance to read the book, David died. I'm so glad now that I created Snowdrift because there is my wonderful father, as a yeti, for everyone to see.

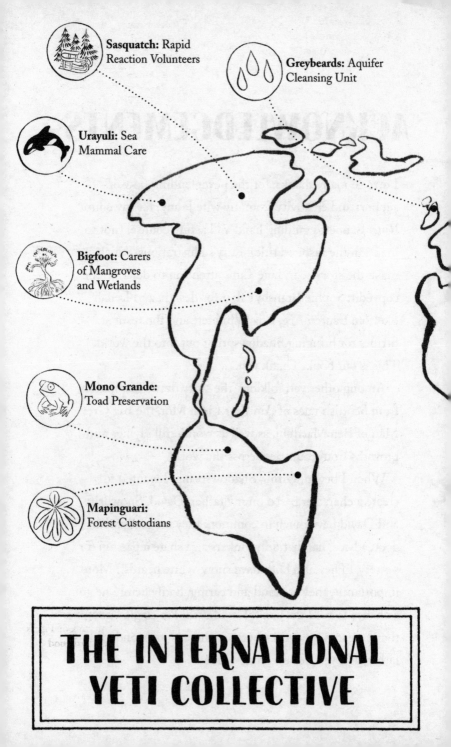

Sasquatch: Rapid Reaction Volunteers

Greybeards: Aquifer Cleansing Unit

Urayuli: Sea Mammal Care

Bigfoot: Carers of Mangroves and Wetlands

Mono Grande: Toad Preservation

Mapinguari: Forest Custodians

THE INTERNATIONAL YETI COLLECTIVE

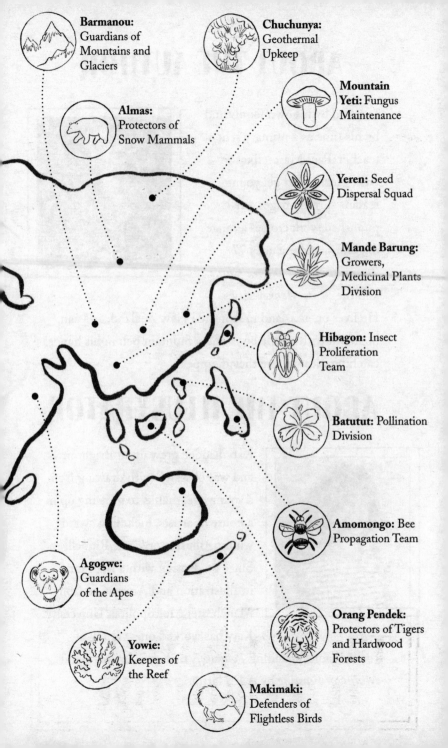

Barmanou: Guardians of Mountains and Glaciers

Chuchunya: Geothermal Upkeep

Almas: Protectors of Snow Mammals

Mountain Yeti: Fungus Maintenance

Yeren: Seed Dispersal Squad

Mande Barung: Growers, Medicinal Plants Division

Hibagon: Insect Proliferation Team

Batutut: Pollination Division

Amomongo: Bee Propagation Team

Agogwe: Guardians of the Apes

Orang Pendek: Protectors of Tigers and Hardwood Forests

Yowie: Keepers of the Reef

Makimaki: Defenders of Flightless Birds

ABOUT THE AUTHOR

Inspired by his own family and by his time as a primary school teacher, Paul Mason likes to write stories that get young readers turning pages. His published work crosses a range of genres, and includes *The Twins, the Ghost and the Castle* and the *Skate Monkey* series.
He lives on an island in Aotearoa New Zealand, and can be found with a little book and a fountain pen in his hands, catching ideas before they disappear.

ABOUT THE ILLUSTRATOR

Katy Riddell grew up in Brighton and was obsessed with drawing from a young age, thanks to growing up in a house of artists, including award-winning illustrator Chris Riddell. Since graduating with a BA Hons in Illustration and Animation from Manchester Metropolitan University, Katy has worked on a variety of commissions including *Pongwiffy* by Kaye Umansky and *Midnight Feasting* by A.F. Harrold.